GOLDIE VANCE™

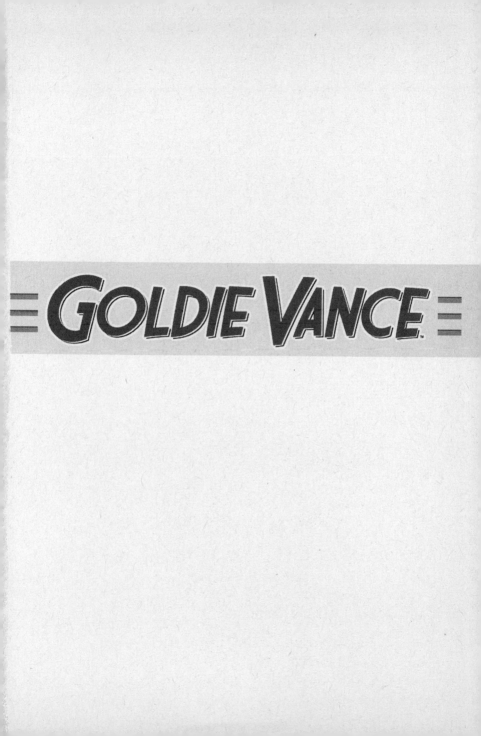

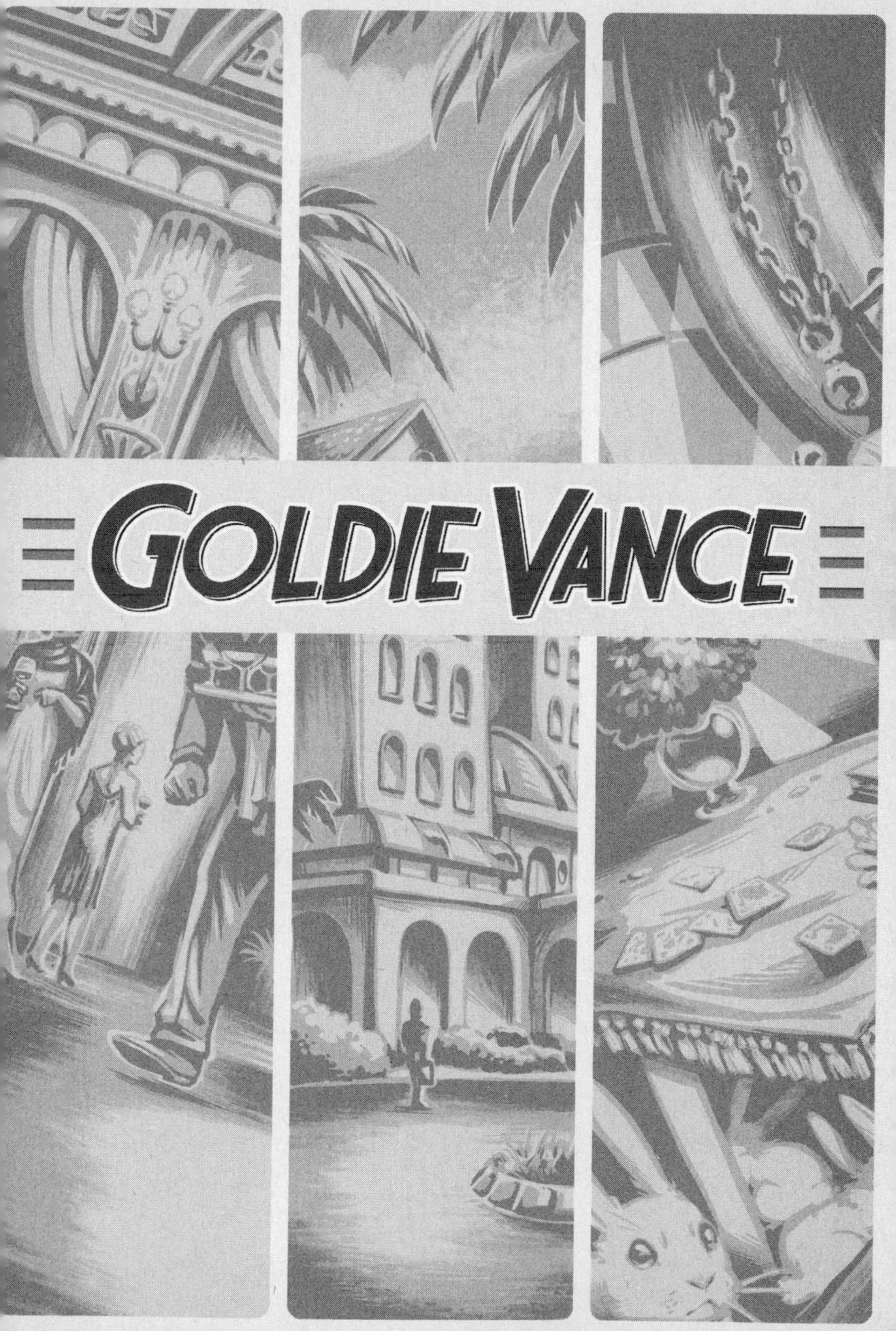
GOLDIE VANCE

Text and Illustration copyright: © 2021 BOOM! Studios **BOOM!** STUDIOS

Goldie Vance™ and © 2021 Hope Larson & Brittney Williams. All rights reserved. BOOM! Studios™ and the BOOM! Studios logo are trademarks of Boom Entertainment, Inc., registered in various countries and categories.

Excerpt from *Goldie Vance: The Hotel Whodunit* copyright © 2020 by BOOM! Studios **BOOM!** STUDIOS

Title page and pattern illustrations by Elle Power
Comic illustrations by Mel Valentine Vargas
Cover illustration by Elle Power

Little, Brown and Company
Hachette Book Group
1290 Avenue of the Americas, New York, NY 10104
Visit us at LBYR.com

First Edition: January 2021

Little, Brown and Company is a division of Hachette Book Group, Inc.
The Little, Brown name and logo are trademarks of Hachette Book Group, Inc.

The publisher is not responsible for websites (or their content) that are not owned by the publisher.

Library of Congress Control Number: 2020947615

ISBNs: 978-0-316-42759-3 (paper over board), 978-0-316-42760-9 (ebook)

Printed in the United States of America

LSC-C

Printing 1, 2020

GOLDIE VANCE

THE HOCUS-POCUS HOAX

An original novel by
Lilliam Rivera

Illustrations by
Elle Power &
Mel Valentine Vargas

Based on the Goldie Vance
comics created by Hope Larson &
Brittney Williams

Little, Brown and Company
New York Boston

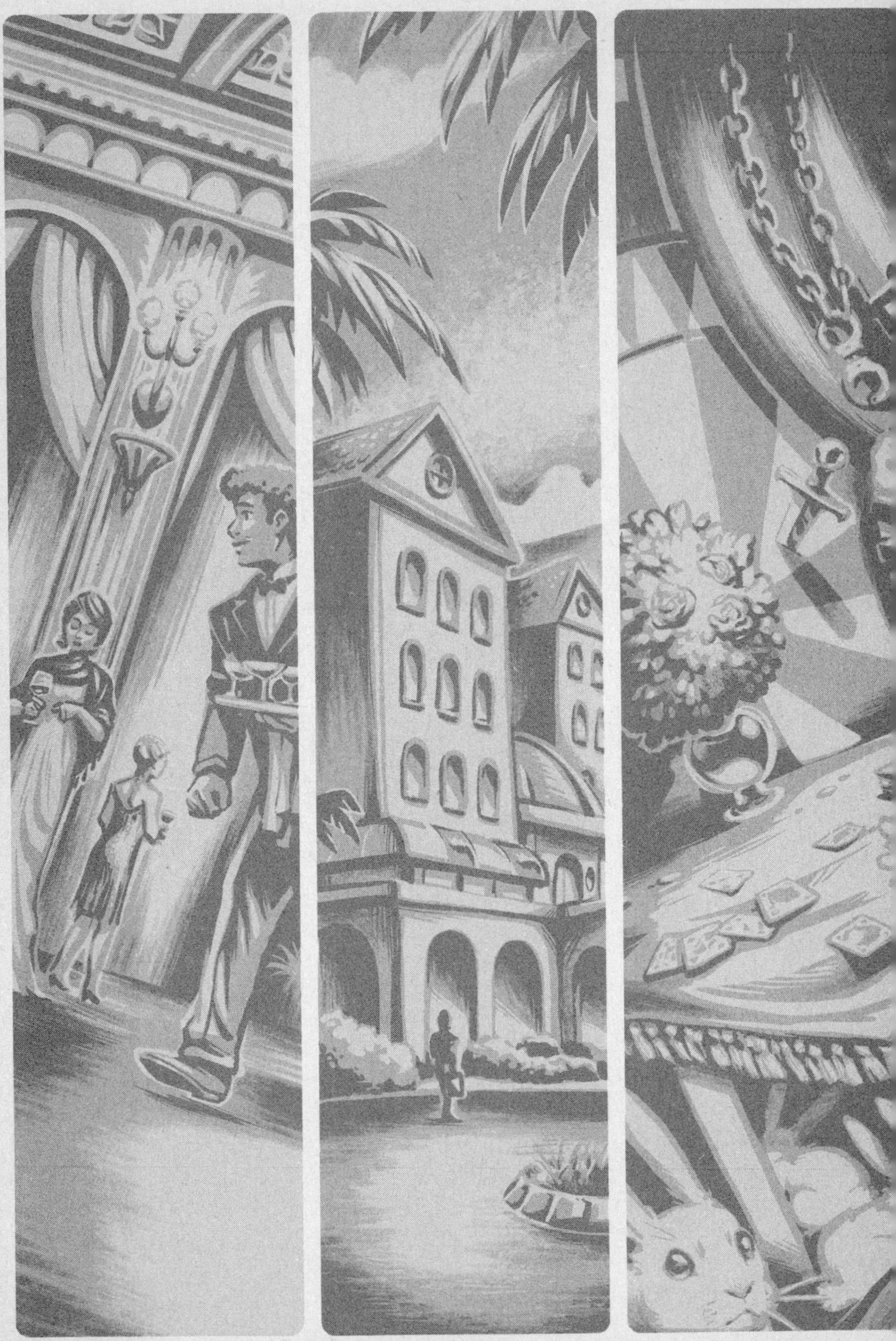

To all the kids
who always look for the
magic in everything

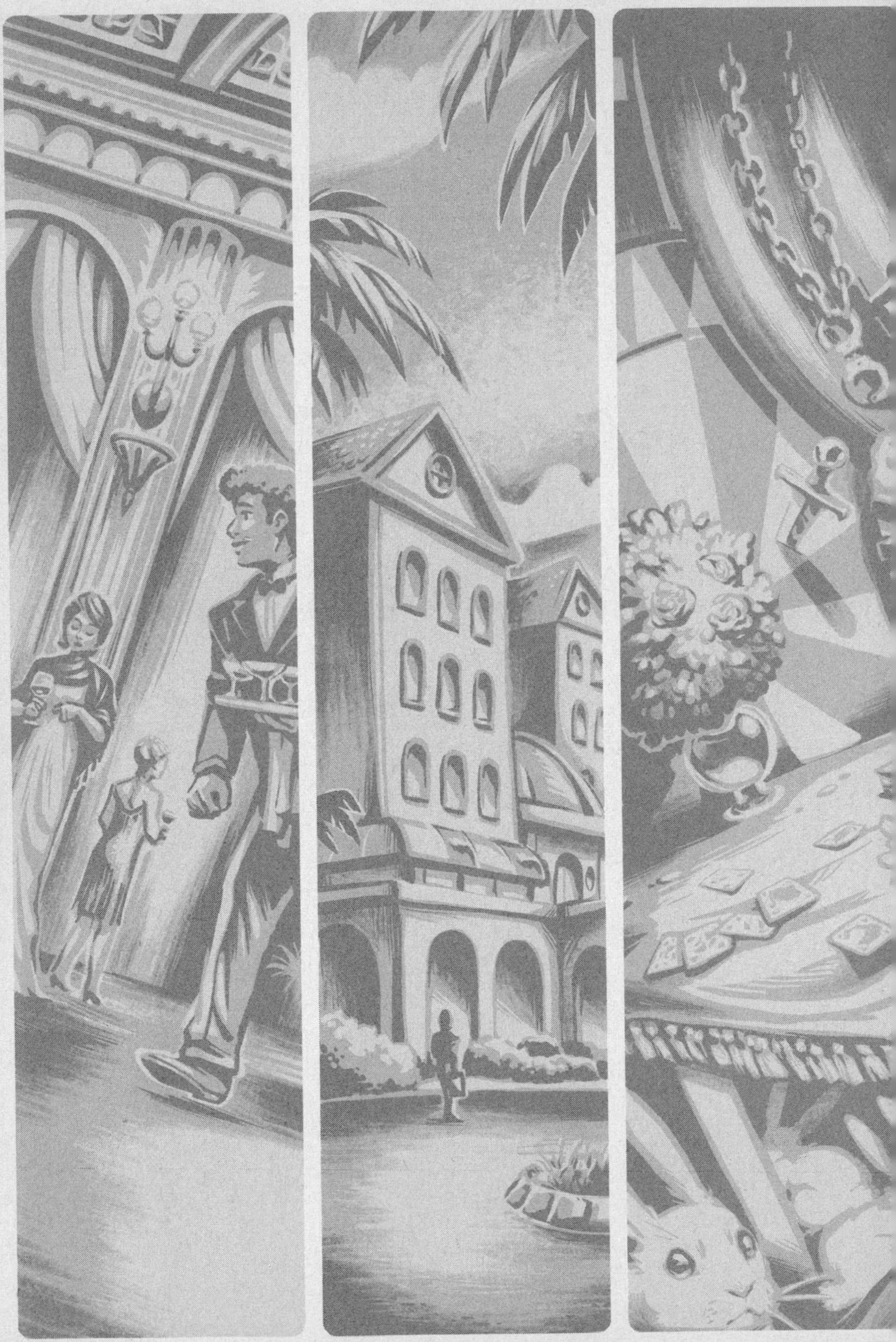

About the Author

Lilliam Rivera is an award-winning writer and author of the young adult novels *Dealing in Dreams* and *The Education of Margot Sanchez*. Her favorite TV detective is Columbo, and she wishes she could be half as smart and adventurous as Goldie! Lilliam lives in Los Angeles, California.

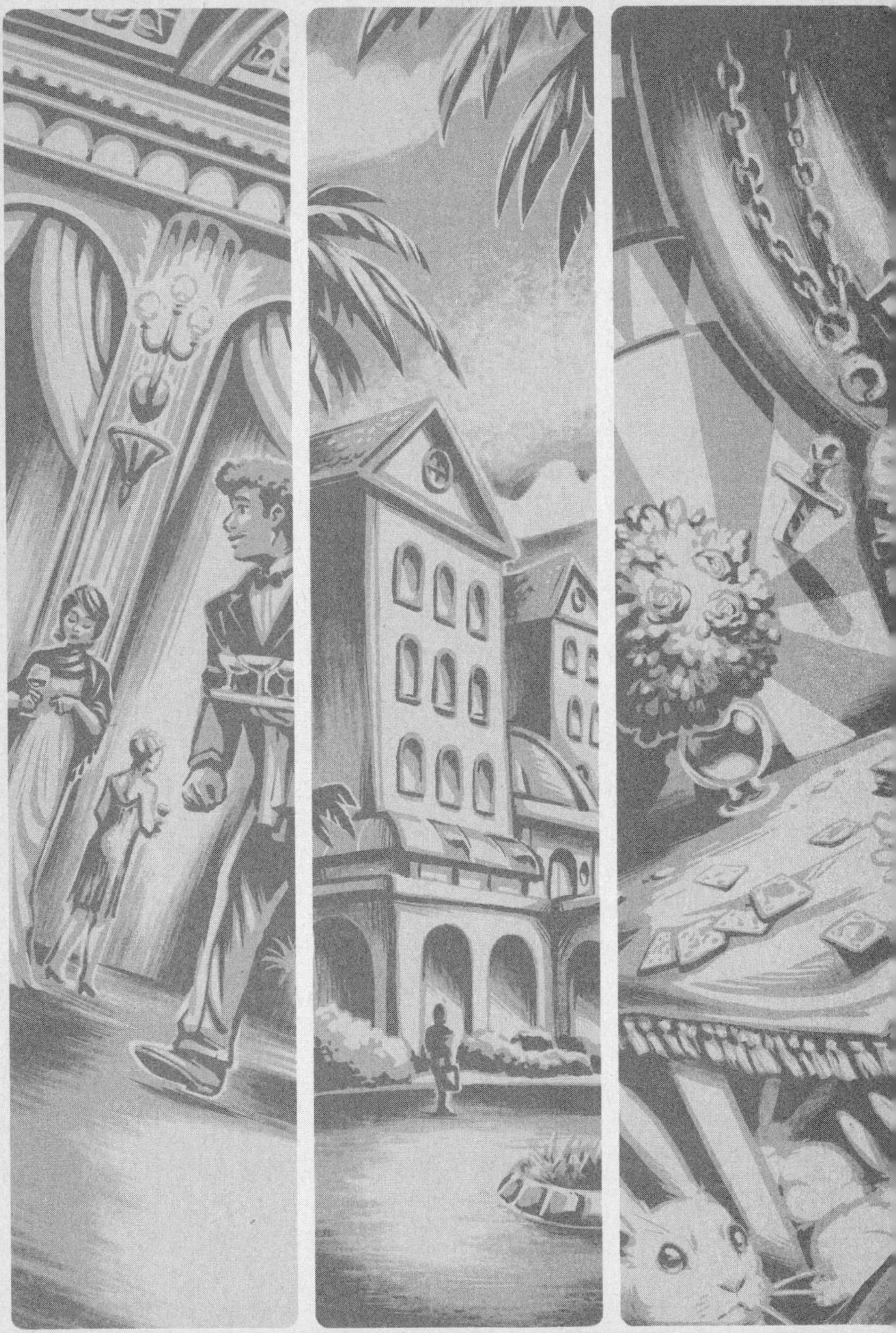

Chapter One

WHEN I WAS A KID, EVERYONE—AND I DO MEAN *everyone*—in my first-grade class was glued to their television screen every Saturday morning to watch the great *Dr. Von Thurston's Magical Hour*. Dr. Von Thurston was by far the biggest thing to hit the tube since *Adventures of Superman*. His commercials promised that his tricks would "dazzle and amaze" viewers of all ages. I had never watched, but I was curious to see what all the hoopla was about. So, one Saturday morning, I asked Dad if I could tune in. He said yes! I ate some delicious waffles and then sat down to watch, excited to take in all the magic.

Well, as the hour came to a close, I didn't feel dazzled *or* amazed. All I could think as Dr. Von Thurston swished around his set in his super-fancy, jewel-encrusted cape and performed his feats of magical wonder was this: He had to be using marked cards! There are only so many tricks you can perform with a *real* deck of cards, so he had to be up to *something* to do all the things he did. But before I could truly close the case, I needed to do some homework.

I spent the rest of the day and night trying to prove this magician was all smoke and mirrors. I found my own deck of cards and attempted to replicate what Dr. Von Thurston did on the small screen. After hours of practice, I came pretty close to figuring out how he was pulling it off. At school on Monday, I shared my findings with the other kids in class, and let's just say they were *not* too happy about it. In fact, their exact words were, "Goldie, why are you such a party pooper?"

And that was my short-lived odyssey into the magical arts. Sigh.

"Can you stop playing with that thing and lend us a hand?"

I snap out of my memory. Cheryl Lebeaux, my best friend and my favorite super genius, is a little annoyed with me at the moment. See, I'm meant to be helping her decorate the ballroom for the League of Magical Arts Convention. Crossed Palms Resort, the place where I work and live, will be the center for illusion-ary tricks, hocus-pocus, and all things sleight of hand, which is pretty cool considering my original take on the magic stuff. That's why I'm standing right outside the ballroom, trying my best to figure out how this woven finger trap actually works. How did my fingers get stuck? It's so bizarre. There is a simple, logical explanation and I aim to figure it out, even if it means losing a digit or two.

"Goldie!"

"Okay, okay. I'll be right with you, Cheryl. Just give me a few seconds," I say as I try to unstick my stuck fingers. "I think I can decode this trick. Maybe I should just cut it open...."

Cheryl is doing what I should be doing. She is neatly placing a woven finger trap on each table set-ting, and there are hundreds of tables.

Earlier this morning, Mr. Maple, our boss and the owner of the Crossed Palms Resort, gathered everyone—hotel staff, valet, custodians, the works—and told us we were all on the League of Magical Arts Convention's welcoming-party committee.

"No fooling around. This is a big account and I don't want any mistakes," Mr. Maple barked. Then he pointed his thick pointer finger at us all to prove he meant business, even though he was looking directly at me, which I found to be a little presumptuous of him. I have every intention to not get distracted or fool around. I'm also not one to make mistakes.

Back in the present, I look down at my stuck digits. "Rob, how do I get my fingers out of this thing?" I ask.

Rob, my other best friend and an expert in the art of valet parking (like *moi*), is at the far end of the ballroom. He's distributing programs next to the place settings.

Rob starts to trot over to where I'm leaning against the long bar. But one quick glance from Cheryl makes him change his mind. Rob has a crush on Cheryl, and Cheryl doesn't believe in goofing off at work. Too bad for Rob. Too bad for Cheryl. And too bad for me and my confounded fingers.

Suddenly, Evan appears from behind the bar. He has shaggy blond hair, a slight build, and a sweet smile. He's been working at Crossed Palms Resort for only a little under six months. He may be a newcomer, but he fits right in, especially when he makes me the sweetest Shirley Temple in town. I know—what's so special about that? Well, Evan adds at least ten cherries and multiple tiny umbrellas, which I love. A fancy drink for a not-so-fancy gal. Now do you get it?

Evan has this lucky coin he's always tossing up in the air. He told me the beautiful gold coin is rare, something he got on a recent trip to Sweden. He's always asking me to guess which side it'll land on—heads or tails. If I guess right, I get another Shirley Temple. Fifty-fifty chances are my type of odds.

"What's the word from the bird?" Evan asks.

"Not much, Evan, just my fingers stuck in this trap," I say. "Do you know anything about these things?"

Evan places a box filled with glasses on the bar and carefully studies my hands. "As a matter of fact, I do." He gently puts his fingers on the link between mine and starts to do some sort of massaging thing. Within seconds, I have my pointer fingers back. Was that magic?

"How did you do that, Evan? I've been trying to wiggle out of this joint for the past thirty minutes with absolutely no luck," I say.

"It's an easy enough trick. Anyone can figure it out," he replies with a shrug.

"While you've been playing around, we've been doing the majority of the work," Cheryl adds as she and Rob join the two of us. She takes my discarded finger trap and places it at the final table setting.

"I wouldn't call what I was doing 'playing.' It was more like sacrificing my pointers for the greater good of the League of Magical Arts Convention's order and business," I say. "Consider my act a generous gift to the welcoming-party committee."

Cheryl places her hands on her hips. She's not quite buying my excuse. That's okay. At least I was able to get away from parking cars, which is technically my job. I can only imagine what that will be like when the magicians finally arrive. Will they hide their car keys and relocate them behind my ears? Will I have to corral bunnies? Will I have to memorize various abracadabras?

"You know, these magicians are just peddling a whole lot of monkey business," Evan says. "If you ask me, the whole convention is a big waste of time."

Wow. Who would have thought sweet, friendly Evan would feel so strongly about the magical arts? Not me.

"No way. This is the best thing that has ever happened to Crossed Palms Resort and St. Pascal," Rob says. "The whole United States, if you ask me."

Rob was in my first-grade class. Not only did he watch *Dr. Von Thurston's Magical Hour* each and every Saturday morning like clockwork, but he also got his parents to buy the Dr. Von Thurston Magic Kit, the Dr. Von Thurston cape, and most important, Dr. Von Thurston's *How to Be a Magician in Thirty Days*. Rob has not stopped talking about the convention ever since Mr. Maple told us about it two months ago. He's a fan, with a capital *F*!

"You too, huh? Charmed by the illusionary arts," Evan says, shaking his head. "Well, don't be. The real trick is that all these people are just hiding behind flashy costumes and glimmering mirrors. Strip that down and you just get someone with a tall story to tell."

Evan returns to the back of the bar, leaving poor Rob looking dejected. I place my arm around his shoulders.

"Forget about him. Soon you'll be in the same hotel as the great Dr. Von Thurston," I say, trying to comfort Rob. "How are you even going to stand it?"

"Yeah," Cheryl chimes in. "Can you believe he's the top headliner of the whole conference?"

Rob's sad expression slides right off his face. "How will I approach him? Should I carry his book with me everywhere so I can tell him how it changed my life and he can sign it? Or maybe I could just try and ask him for some advice.... What do you think?"

Cheryl shakes her head. "The first thing Mr. Maple said to me this morning was, 'Make sure no one bothers the headliners.' That definitely includes you, Rob."

Rob scratches his head. Poor guy. This is his big chance to meet his hero. I decide right then and there to help him achieve his goal. That's what friends are for.

"What's on the agenda?" I ask.

Cheryl gathers her clipboard of very important notes. More than 3,500 budding and world-famous magicians will be converging on the resort within hours to attend this conference. Cheryl says the convention was planned ages ago and attendees have traveled from across the country to be here. It's the biggest magic convention in the US, and Mr. Maple has apparently been courting it for years. Now that we've finally gotten it, every establishment in St. Pascal has gone full-on *alakazam*. Restaurants have transformed their menus to include "bewitching burgers." My favorite fruit stand right off the highway has started putting out ads that say, *Levitate Your Date!*

"After this, I'm set to meet with the organizers of

the convention to go over the seating chart one more time," Cheryl says. "There are so many opinions on which mentalist should sit with which conjuror. I didn't even know there was a difference."

"Well, actually, there is a very important distinction between—"

Cheryl raises her hand to stop Rob from explaining.

"I'm doing it again, ain't I?" he says sheepishly. "Sorry, I can't help it. I guess I'm excited."

I chuckle. Rob has gotten into serious tangents about magic tricks and magician lingo before. The detours are super useful when Cheryl has to help the chef come up with a new themed menu but are not as helpful after we've heard him explain the linking-rings illusion five hundred times.

Rob, Cheryl, and I lean against the bar and survey the completed setup. The Sugar Maple Ballroom is named after Mr. Maple's daughter, Sugar, who I refuse to discuss at any length. She's my archnemesis, though she wasn't always my enemy. We used to be the best of friends. I even have pictures of us laughing and playing. Then...I'm not sure what happened. She just became super competitive with me and, ugh—Sugar can be such a meanie. One time she...

Oops. I digress.

Anyway, my favorite longtime hotel resident, Miss Dupart, likes to say, "Darling, if they are expending so much energy on you, they must be very attuned to your divine glow." Can you believe it? My divine glow? I didn't even know I had a glow, let alone one that's enchanting the world. Miss Dupart knows all there is to know about glow—she used to be a famous Hollywood star! Now she's a Crossed Palms Resort resident who spends most of her time lounging with her trusty sidekick, her tiny poodle, Clementine. Miss Dupart is the best.

The Sugar Maple Ballroom is one of three ballrooms in the hotel. When you enter it, the first thing you notice is the massive chandelier overtaking the center of the ceiling. Each crystal on the chandelier is brilliant and sparkles like a diamond. The chandelier lights up the room and is quite a wonder. Even though the other two ballrooms are much smaller, they're still just as glorious.

"I think we did a great job," I say.

"We?" Cheryl and Rob ask simultaneously.

"I helped! Now I can totally vouch that the woven finger trap works," I say defensively. "The magicians are experts. They're not going to accept just any old party favor. Wouldn't you agree?"

Cheryl nudges me a little with her shoulder.

"You're right," she admits.

"Is your date with Diane still happening today?" Rob asks.

Finally! A topic that's truly magical in every sense of the word. I can't help letting out a long, swoony sigh. I'm positive my peepers look like big ol' thumping hearts right now.

Diane works at Wax Lips, the record store, and she's the most beautiful person in St. Pascal. She has short hair, she sometimes models, and she has a love for striped shirts. Did I mention how beautiful she is? I've always crushed on her from afar, but I recently took my crush to the next level. I asked her to have dinner with me, and she said yes!

"Yup. This is our *official* official first date," I say, feeling myself getting just slightly flustered. "We've hung out at Wax Lips a couple of times, we've listened to music, and boy, can she drive a getaway car! But today is different."

Cheryl adjusts one of the plate settings. "Where did you finally decide to go?"

"I'm taking you up on your advice and going somewhere nice. We have reservations at Josephine's for dinner."

"With music! Don't forget the music," Cheryl says. "A violin player visits each table and serenades the guests. It's very romantic."

My cheesy grin gets even cheesier.

"Wow, you're really going all out, huh, Goldie?" Rob asks.

"The restaurant overlooks the ocean, so maybe we can take a walk afterward." Then I pause. "Is that too much?"

"It's kind of funny to see you this way, Goldie," Rob says. "I don't think I've ever seen you so nervous in all my life."

Oh my goodness. Rob is right. I've got to pull myself together. I fix my yellow headband and pull down my uniform's sweater-vest. My face is burning up. Rob and Cheryl exchange bemused looks. I try my best to shake off my nerves. I'm at work. I can't let thoughts of Diane distract me.

And that's when I start to hear something.

"Hey, do you hear that?" I ask. Both of them shake

their heads, but I can totally pick up something out of the ordinary. It's a low rumbling, as if a train is heading straight toward the ballroom.

"Listen," I insist. Cheryl and Rob strain their ears. They even lean forward. Still nothing. Then I notice the table.

I point to the glasses. They're trembling and making clinking sounds that are getting increasingly loud. It can't be an earthquake. St. Pascal rarely gets them because we're a tropical town. Hurricanes and heat waves are more our speed. But this is a different type of storm. A man-made one.

"Oh boy." Rob finally hears it. He eyes the door, but there's no time for a quick escape. My calculations tell me we might as well face whoever is about to enter the Sugar Maple Ballroom. We get ready, our hands by our sides.

Evan appears with another box of glasses. Rob shakes his head at him, and Evan stashes the box away and pulls a rag from behind the counter to give the bar a quick polish.

The noise gets louder. The train is approaching the station.

"Ready?" Cheryl asks. We nod.

We brace ourselves as the vibrations shaking the dishes on the tables get more violent. This can mean one thing and one thing only.

"What's going on in here?!" Mr. Maple bellows as he enters the ballroom.

Chapter Two

THE OWNER OF THE CROSSED PALMS RESORT STORMS into the ballroom like a Category 2 hurricane. His dedicated and patient secretary walks behind him, as does a whole entourage of people. Mr. Maple rarely leaves his office. When he does, he usually travels with a crowd. I like to call them his pencil-pushing gang, but Dad is not too keen on me using the word *gang*. The pencil-pushing gang—hotel-office people—gives me the "look." The "look" is a warning every employee at the Crossed Palms Resort learns as soon as they start working here. It's used to alert everyone in the surrounding area that Mr. Maple is in rare form.

"Mr. Maple, we're just about done with the ballroom," Cheryl says. She clasps the clipboard to her chest, almost like a shield. It's times like these I try to yield the floor to Cheryl. She often works closely with Mr. Maple and his massive entourage. I rarely get the pleasure because I'm usually busy parking cars. Even though I'm good at it, everyone knows what I really want to be is the house detective. I've been training my whole life, ever since Mom gave me my first magnifying glass when I was seven.

"Humph," Mr. Maple grunts. He strolls steadily around the tables, inspecting our work. I get an itchy feeling inside, an urge to say something. It's hard to suppress it but I must, especially since Mr. Maple's entourage contains two very important people. First is the hotel's actual house detective, Walter Tooey, who's currently looking a bit nervous and wiping a bead of sweat from his brow. Walt is my mentor, and I'm his assistant. In between parking cars, I help him solve mysteries. Walt says I have a good eye for it. And I do! Just the other week I helped solve the case of the missing Bejeweled Aqua Chapeau, and then there was the case with that Soviet spy. It was kind of a big deal, which I guess makes me kind of a big deal, too.

"Hi, Walt!" I say, waving. He in turn flashes me the

"look." I respond with a grin. Walt does not return my smile. As Rob said just minutes ago, *Oh boy*.

Right behind Walt is my dear ol' dad. Dad is the manager of the Crossed Palms Resort. He's really good at what he does. He's patient and calm, the two things you need when working at a very busy and popular resort. There's always a crisis that needs to be averted, and Dad does so with ease.

Dad sees me and gives me a wink, which is all it takes to make me feel better.

"You!" Mr. Maple points to Evan.

"Yes, sir?"

"These are very important clients," Mr. Maple barks. "When table one is seated, make sure the drinks are flowing, and don't skimp on the powerful stuff. I don't care about the rest of the tables. Keep your eye on table one."

"Yes, sir. I'll make sure the glasses are filled to the brim on table one," Evan says. "Any special drink orders?"

Mr. Maple swivels over to his crowd of people pleasers, and they start to whisper among themselves until his secretary eventually steps forward. She whispers something to my dad, who also steps out of the blob of people.

"Dr. Von Thurston is set to be seated at table one like you requested, Mr. Maple," Dad says.

"Well, of course he is!" Mr. Maple yells. "Dr. Von Thompson is the top headliner. Where else would he sit?"

"It's Von Thurston," I say.

My comment hushes the entourage. You can practically hear Walt's heart thrumming against his rib cage. *No one* corrects Mr. Maple, especially not a short girl with a yellow headband.

"That's what I said—Von Thurston," Mr. Maple says, totally ignoring my existence. Then he goes right back to addressing the whole ballroom. "What about it?"

"He will only drink iced tea with a slice of lime," Dad says.

"Then make sure he gets his iced tea!"

Evan nods and goes back to standing like a statue behind the bar. Mr. Maple continues his inspection.

"What is this here? What is this?" Mr. Maple picks up a woven finger trap and everyone freezes again. I see Cheryl grimace while Rob stares at the carpeted floor. When no one pipes up, Mr. Maple prods again. "Well?"

"I would be careful if I were you, Mr. Maple," I say, breaking formation to walk over to him. "It's a woven finger trap, and I spent the last half hour trying to extract my stuck fingers. If you look closely, you can see it's still red."

I show him my finger, and Mr. Maple steps back as if I'd shown him a broken body part.

"Whose idea was this?"

Now it's Cheryl's turn to step up to the plate.

"The League of Magical Arts sent us party favors," she says. "They wanted to make sure the guests leave with a little token for their continued support."

"A trick?" Mr. Maple says with disgust.

At the far end of the ballroom, the doors swing wide open.

"Good morning!"

Angela Diaz enters, wearing a pretty, yellow fit-and-flare dress. "I'm ready for my close-up, Mr. DeMille."

Angela Diaz goes by the name of Angela, the Sorceress of Wonder, and she's St. Pascal's very own magician. I love watching her work. Angela tells me it's rare to see a female magician grace the stage.

Women are usually relegated to assistant positions, but the Sorceress of Wonder comes from a *long* line of magicians, so she accepts nothing less. Her father is a magician. Her grandfather is, too. As a kid, Angela toured the states with her family, performing at various festivals and county fairs. Her father now owns a small magic shop here in town, where you can pick up all types of tricks. It's a pretty fun shop.

Angela is set to entertain the group tonight.

"Where would you like me to be?" Angela asks in a boisterous yet blunt tone that doesn't quite match her petite frame but immediately turns heads. I think Angela's real trick is how she appears meek and demure offstage but commands attention onstage and backstage. She loves performing in glamorous gowns, and her signature act includes beautiful doves that magically appear out of thin air. I ask her how she does it all the time. But true to the magician's code, Angela never tells. She doesn't even give me a hint.

"We're almost done here, and then we'll be able to do the rundown of your show," Dad says. "Just a few more minutes."

"Whatever you say."

Angela tugs a chair from one of the tables, sits down, and pulls a deck of cards from her pocket. She smiles at me before she starts to shuffle.

After a few strolls around the ballroom, Mr. Maple seems content enough with the decorations. Cheryl lets out a sigh of relief as Mr. Maple and his entourage gather themselves to head to the exit.

Just when Mr. Maple is finally about to leave, a bellboy runs into the ballroom, out of breath. He walks over to Dad and whispers in his ear.

"Are you sure about that?" Dad asks. "Ummm, Mr. Maple, there seems to be an issue."

Mr. Maple places his hand on the door. Cheryl moans quietly beside me. This can't be good.

"It appears three of our servers have contracted the stomach flu. We will be short-staffed tonight."

"Short-staffed!" Mr. Maple yells. "Short-staffed. That won't do!"

He turns around and his eyes land on us.

"You two." Mr. Maple points to Cheryl and then to me. Rob tries to hide behind me, which is ridiculous. He's bigger than I am. "And you. You are now on for tonight."

I can't work today. This totally can't happen to me.

I'm not scheduled to work tonight. He can't do this. Please, no.

"Excuse me, Mr. Maple," I say. Doesn't he understand I have a very important date with Diane? I plead with him. "I can't possibly work tonight. I have a date."

Mr. Maple twirls like a tornado to face me directly.

"Excuse me? You didn't actually just tell me you can't work tonight because of a date, did you?" he asks.

Walt is giving me the "look." Cheryl is giving me the "look." Heck, even *Dad* is giving me the "look."

I sigh dejectedly. "No, Mr. Maple, I didn't...."

"This is a Crossed Palms Resort team effort. Everyone's on deck!"

"Yes, Mr. Maple."

With that, Mr. Maple and most of the entourage walk out of the ballroom. Dad stays behind.

"Sorry, Goldie," he says. "You'll have to reschedule your plans."

He gives me a quick hug before trotting off to join the rest of the pencil-pushing gang. I slump into a chair beside Angela. I can't believe it. My first official date with Diane is over before it could even get started.

"And I thought I had it made in the shade," I say.

Rob and Cheryl gather round, offering me condolences.

"Sorry about that, Goldie. But does this mean I'll be in the same room as *the* Dr. Von Thurston? And do I have to wear a *tux*?" Rob asks. "It's my least favorite part of being a valet. I hate bow ties."

"We'll not only have to wear bow ties, but we'll also have to make sure the drinks are flowing on table one. What a nightmare!" Cheryl jots down the changes to the schedule on her agenda. "I gotta alert the rest of the staff."

Cheryl runs off, leaving me to mend my broken heart.

"Sorry, kid. As they always say in the biz, the show must go on," Angela says. She spreads her deck of cards in front of me. "Pick a card. Any card. Make sure not to show me."

I do. To my surprise, it's the queen of hearts.

"Now put the card back, anywhere you want."

I do.

"Now try to think about your card. Make sure you tell me your card, telepathically, so it will connect to my noggin right here."

Angela taps her forehead. I close my eyes.

"Tails, you pull out the wrong card," Evan says, and he flips his lucky coin up in the air and catches it.

"Aren't you the nonbeliever?" Angela says. "I don't think we've met."

"Evan, this is Angela. Angela, Evan." Rob does the introductions.

"Now, is this your card?" Angela asks.

She pulls out a joker, and I can't help appreciating the irony. This is a complete joke, my having to work. But it's the wrong card. I shake my head.

"Of course not. That's not what you are magnetically sending to me." Angela closes her eyes. "No. No. No."

She opens her eyes wide. "Actually, Rob, can you check your pockets? I think you have something that belongs to me."

Rob quickly does as he's told and discovers the queen of hearts in his left pocket. He gasps.

"I love this trick!" Rob exclaims.

"Magicians." Evan snorts behind us and tucks his coin away.

It's a great trick. It is! But it doesn't erase the fact I'll have to let Diane down.

Seeing my frown, Angela does a bit of a flourish with her hands and makes a rose appear out of thin air.

"Here you go, sweet Goldie."

"Thanks." I hold the rose to my nose and think of Diane.

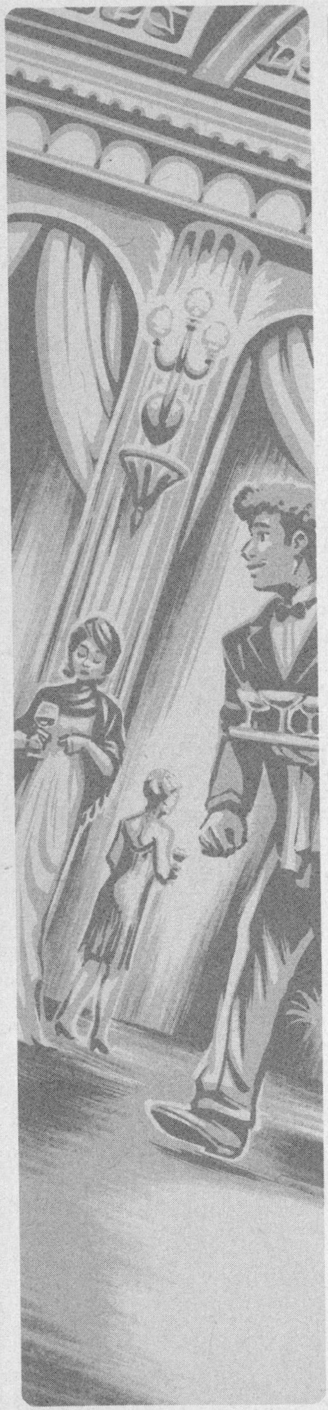
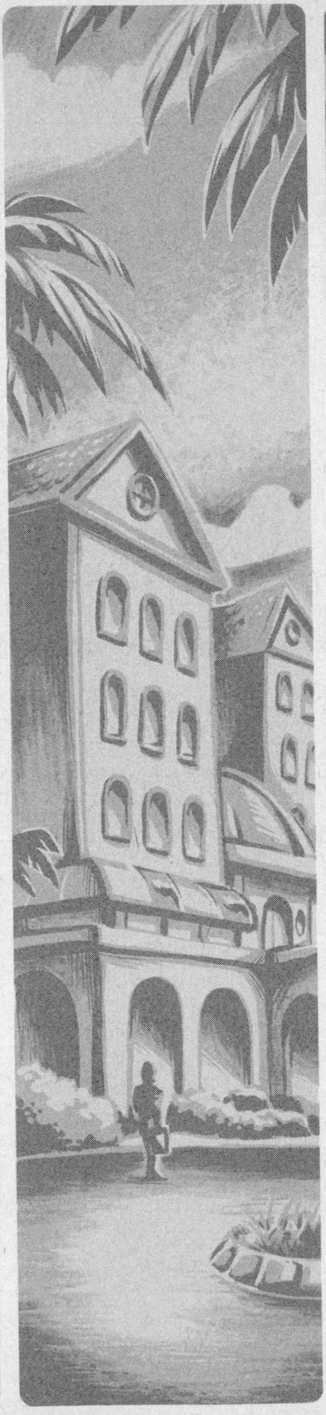
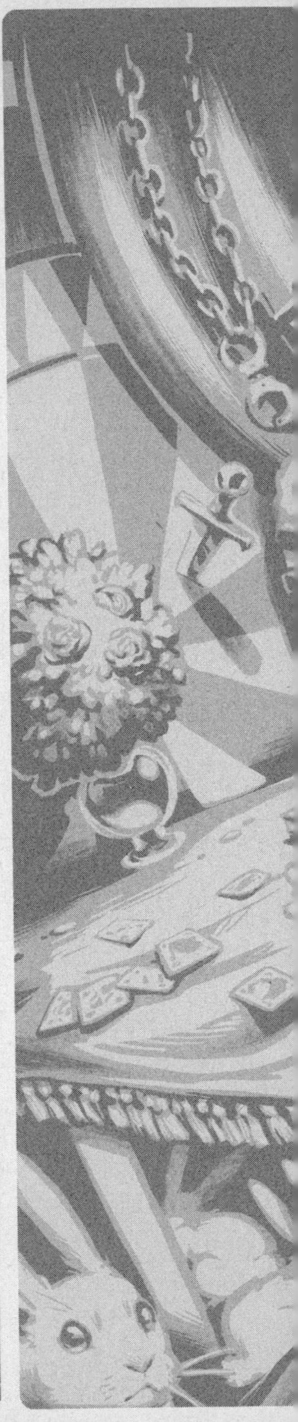

Chapter Three

ꟼ THINK MY BOW TIE IS TRYING TO STRANGLE ME.

"I don't know about this, Cheryl," I say, trying to loosen it up. It's so tight and the outfit goes against my whole fashion persona. I live for chinos and sweater-vests. These tuxes are just way too stiff. My magnifying glass can barely fit in the pants pockets!

"Stop fiddling," Cheryl says. "You look great!"

"Well, at least your suit fits you," Rob says. "Look at me!"

Rob had to borrow a tuxedo from the regular staff. We all did. Unfortunately, his jacket is a size too small, and there wasn't enough time for us to find a more suitable replacement.

"Just leave it unbuttoned and make sure to move

quickly whenever you get too close to Mr. Maple," Cheryl says.

She walks over to Rob and straightens his tie. Cheryl and Rob smile at each other. They're cute, but I'm reminded of my love predicament and get sad.

Earlier in the day, I had to call Diane at Wax Lips to cancel our date.

"It's okay. We'll try again soon," she said.

Her reaction sprung hope and made me even more determined. I promised her I would reschedule the dinner reservations for tomorrow. I can't be on call *all* weekend long. Aren't there laws against working a person to the bone?

"I need to button this jacket because I don't want anyone to see this."

Rob opens his shirt to reveal his copy of Dr. Von Thurston's *How to Be a Magician in Thirty Days*. No wonder his suit jacket won't close!

"I figured when there's a lull in my shift, I might be able to get his signature," Rob says sheepishly.

"Smart," I say. "See, I have my pad and pen, just in case." I show them my tools so Rob doesn't feel as embarrassed. *Always be prepared* is my personal motto.

"Our job is to serve food to these magicians, not to see if they're up to any foul play or to bother them for autographs," Cheryl says. "Can you both promise to focus? I don't want Mr. Maple to get mad at us."

"No sweat! We'll blend in like the rest of the penguins," I say. "Just us penguins serving food. Waddle. Waddle. Waddle."

I do my best penguin impression and Rob follows my lead. Cheryl laughs. Soon, three penguins are waddling in the kitchen. As much as Chef François, the Crossed Palms Resort's head of culinary everything, is happy to see us working tonight, he's not super excited about penguins waddling in his place of work. He flashes us a look, which is not to be confused with *the* "look." This one is more of a universal "cut it out." We stop.

The doors to the ballroom haven't been officially opened, but they will be soon. In the meantime, the sweet aroma of Chef François's amazing cooking is making my stomach growl and my eyes water.

"*Petite fille*, would you like to try one?" asks Chef François in his awesome French accent.

"*Oui*," I say.

He offers a tray of French cheese puffs, or *gougères*,

as he calls them. I eat one and immediately want to store another in my pocket for later. A little cheese puff can do wonders for a person. After two quick bites, the tux doesn't feel so bad. It also reminds me that I *do* get to work with my two best friends tonight.

The cooks are lining up the trays of various snacks that we'll be circulating to the crowd of magicians before they take their assigned seats. Chef François runs a very tight kitchen. If you're ever lucky enough to find yourself in a kitchen as professional as the one in the Crossed Palms Resort, you'll see a true work of art. Every single person has a job to do, and they do it with precision and love. Like a dance, the cooks work in unison, calling out to one another if someone is missing an ingredient or a garnish of any type. I can watch them work all day, especially if I get to sample the wares.

Just as I'm about to pop another one of the cheesy cheese puffs, a bell goes off. It's our cue to take the many delicious treats out to the ballroom.

"All right, penguins," I say as I grab a tray. "Let's go waddle with the magicians!"

The Sugar Maple Ballroom is slowly filling up with pretty dresses, suits, and dazzling capes. It's a slow surge and not too intense. People are making their way in, matching their names with their assigned seats. Rob is beside himself with excitement. I bet I would feel just like he does if I were in a ballroom filled with detectives. Just imagine the possibilities. We could exchange detective tips, like, What are the best gadgets to use? The appropriate binoculars? Huh, maybe I should push for a detective convention. Does that even exist? Mental note to find out.

Speaking of detectives, Walt is here. Like a good detective, he totally blends in: He's wearing a tux, like the rest of the staff. Nothing out of the ordinary in his attire. I mosey over to him while guests grab cheese puffs off my tray.

"Care for a *gougère*?" I ask.

Walt shakes his head. "No eating while on the job."

"Don't worry, Walt. I'm following the detective rules even though I'm starving," I say. "Anything I should be paying attention to?"

I scan the ballroom like Walt. As a detective, your eyeballs should always be moving. It's quite a skill to pay attention to a conversation while tracking the actions of those around.

"This is just your standard observation. You know

the drill. Survey the room for any unusual occurrences." Walt tugs a bit at his tie. "You just stick to making sure these guests are well fed and the iced tea flows."

"Flowing iced tea," I say. "Got it!"

The key to being a strong detective is being a keen observer. For example, as I walk across the ballroom, offering cheese puffs to guests, I notice a magician pulling a coin from behind a young woman's ear. Next to him is another magician, not impressed by the trick. But the woman sure is. She is laughing with glee. Is the frowning magician jealous, is he a rival, or is this his usual demeanor and my first reaction isn't quite right? As a detective, you have to consider all the possibilities, make a note of them, and press on.

When I run out of cheese puffs, I head back to the kitchen to reload. This time Chef François hands me a tray of salmon mousse canapés.

"Salmon canapés? Salmon canapés?" I say as the ballroom becomes more and more crowded. I spy Angela Diaz commanding a group of people. Rob is across the way, looking nervously at the ballroom doors. He's waiting for Dr. Von Thurston to appear. Cheryl is off helping a group of guests find their seats, while Walt cases the room. Everything is moving along.

"Do you have anything else besides canapés? How about pigs in a blanket or fondue? Don't you have fondue?"

A boy about my age with curly dark-brown hair is suddenly standing beside me, asking questions at a rapid speed. Unlike the rest of the attendees, he's not dressed in a tux. Instead, this boy wears a bright-blue velvet suit.

"No, we don't have any fondue. Would you like to try the salmon canapés?"

"Salmon canapés are a major snafu. The last convention we attended struck canapés off the menu and ordered extra pigs in a blanket," he says. "People may scoff at pigs in a blanket, but why meddle with a good thing? That's what I always say."

I nod at him, smile, and walk over to another group. To my surprise, Blue Velvet Suit follows me. I'm not sure what's happening. Maybe he's bored and wants to continue to extol the virtues of pigs in a blanket? I can't say.

"Fondue is the epitome of gourmet cooking right now," he says.

"I'll make sure to relay the message to the chef," I say. "Now, if you'll excuse me."

I take a few steps. He follows. "If you hold the tray on your right-hand side, you'll be able to navigate this crowd better. Like this." Before I can stop him, he grabs my tray and starts to prove his point by hoisting it over his right shoulder. A guest takes a canapé from the tray.

"Excuse me! My job is to serve *you*," I say, pulling the tray away from him. "Not the other way around."

"Don't get bent out of shape. Just trying to help."

What is Blue Velvet Suit talking about? I'm doing a great job. I give him a curt nod and stomp back to the kitchen.

"I can't believe it. The nerve of that guy!" I huff as I pass through the doors.

Cheryl is right behind me, about to grab a tray of food. "Who are you talking about?"

"The one in the velvet suit. Have you seen him? He won't stop telling me about fondue and pigs in a blanket. He really teed me off." We look through the circular window, and I point to Blue Velvet Suit. "That guy!"

"Nice suit," Cheryl says.

"Well, yeah, of course he's wearing a nice suit. It's the words coming out of his mouth that have me blowing my cool," I explain.

"He's probably just trying to be helpful, that's all." Cheryl shrugs.

"Funny. That's basically what he said to me."

Another bell rings to alert the guests it's time to sit down for dinner. We each grab a pitcher of water and head out. I try my best to ignore Blue Velvet Suit, which is not an easy task. He keeps finding excuses to be by my side, offering unsolicited advice on the best way to pour a glass of water.

"And you don't want to pour too many ice cubes because it makes it really difficult for a person to enjoy their drink," he says.

"Thanks!" I say with a big smile, although what I really want to do is pour this pitcher over his head. But that's not the Crossed Palms way. I take a deep breath and carry on. I won't have a cow. Maybe he just can't help himself. Who am I to judge?

I continue to fill glasses as he rattles on about tap water versus mountain spring water. I simply nod politely.

Luckily, Blue Velvet Suit's running of the mouth is interrupted when Rob heads over to us. "He's here!" he says breathlessly.

I look toward the door and see that a huge crowd of guests have left their seats to gravitate around a cloaked figure. The whole room is abuzz with excitement now, not just Rob. Every single person in the ballroom is on their toes, trying to get a glimpse. There is absolutely no question—Dr. Von Thurston has entered the Sugar Maple Ballroom.

"Make way, people!"

Mr. Maple tries to take control of the scene, but even he is no match for these fired-up Dr. Von Thurston fans.

"The hotel should have hired a dedicated security detail." Blue Velvet Suit is back at it. "Dr. Von Thurston is the greatest magician of all time. He's smart, brilliant—some would even say a legend. You simply can't expect him to enter a room and not be accosted."

"You seem to know a lot about Dr. Von Thurston," I say.

"Of course I do. Don't you?" he asks. "Isn't it your job to know about the guests at your hotel?"

Why does Blue Velvet Suit feel so compelled to explain things to me? I would just ignore him in normal circumstances, but he's a guest, so I turn things around and ask him questions.

"Do you need help finding your seat number?" I

ask, hoping it will deter him. "Cheryl would be more than happy to assist you."

Cheryl walks over to us with the biggest smile. "I sure would. How can I help?"

"You can't. Whoever made these seat assignments should have paid closer attention to where Dr. Von Thurston prefers to sit," Blue Velvet Suit says. Cheryl's smile slowly dissolves. "His best angle is his right side, and these seats are not facing the correct direction."

Now Cheryl sees what I've been complaining about. Rob, on the other hand, doesn't seem fazed by what Blue Velvet Suit's said. Not one bit.

"Do you think we should move the tables?" Rob asks. "We don't want Dr. Von Thurston to be seen from his bad side, do we?"

Cheryl glares at Rob for a full minute. She's been working nonstop to figure out the best seating arrangements. To rearrange them now would be a disaster.

"It's too late," Blue Velvet Suit says. "Dr. Von Thurston doesn't believe in sudden changes. He says it disturbs his equilibrium."

This guy takes being a fan to a whole new level.

"How could you possibly know so much about Dr. Von Thurston?" I ask.

Cheryl and Rob tilt their heads to the side, waiting for his answer.

"Isn't it obvious?" Blue Velvet Suit replies. "He's my father."

Rob gasps and then starts coughing uncontrollably.

"Dr. Von Thurston is your dad?!" Rob exclaims. "How did I not know that?"

"I should probably take my rightful seat. Here's my card."

Blue Velvet Suit digs in his pocket and hands me a business card. The crowd has somewhat dissipated by this point, so he walks over to Dr. Von Thurston's table and takes the seat to his father's right. I hear Dr. Von Thurston proclaim to his tablemates how talented his son is.

When I finally gather my jaw off the floor, I read the card he gave me.

DEREK VON THURSTON

PART-TIME MAGICIAN/PART-TIME DETECTIVE

FULL-TIME EXPERT

Part-time detective?!

Chapter Four

I CAN'T BELIEVE IT. BLUE VELVET SUIT IS DR. VON Thurston's son. I'm not sure whether I should be flattered he wanted to explain things to me or just as annoyed. I think I'm sticking to the latter.

"Wow. We've been standing here talking to Dr. Von Thurston's son the whole time?" Rob says, unable to contain his excitement. "We practically rubbed elbows with the legend himself. We are *this close* to a genius."

As the guests start to settle in again, we diligently wait for Evan, who is busy as ever, to fill our pitchers. Rob stares longingly at Dr. Von Thurston.

"What if I serve table one?" Rob asks. Both Cheryl and I shake our heads. As much as I want Rob to meet his idol, I'm worried he'll trip and pour iced tea all over the magician's face.

"I don't know, Rob," Cheryl says. "You might get nervous."

"You're probably right," he says. "I'll just wait for a better opportunity. Now that Goldie's pals with Derek Von Thurston, I'm sure I'll be exchanging charming stories with Dr. Von Thurston in no time."

I hate to burst Rob's bubble. I am definitely not "pals" with Derek. Not even one bit. Once our pitchers are filled, we head back into the now-seated crowd.

A man wearing a top hat has taken the stage. He welcomes the guests with a story about the League of Magical Arts and how membership has grown from a paltry five magicians meeting in a basement to thousands worldwide. I can't help being impressed that so many people love magic enough to meet like this to perfect their art and exchange ideas. I wish again that there were a detective club where I could connect with like-minded sleuths.

I lean over a woman seated at table one and fill her glass. Derek nods at me. I hope he's not planning on also teaching me the proper way to pour iced tea. Thankfully, he doesn't seem to want to interrupt his dad. Dr. Von Thurston is ignoring the current speaker onstage and telling a very long tale about the first time he performed a magic trick. Those seated at the table are completely enraptured by Dr. Von Thurston, including Mr. Maple.

"I was only five years old. Even back then I knew the magical arts were my true calling," Dr. Von Thurston says with an emphatic nod. "I've never once turned my back to it."

I fill Dr. Von Thurston's glass with iced tea. As soon as I pull away, he drinks the whole glass and nods for me to fill it again.

"What do you think about St. Pascal?" a lady wearing a giant feathered hat asks. Mr. Maple leans forward.

"It's very quaint. It has a certain je ne sais quoi," Dr. Von Thurston says. "Charming."

Mr. Maple sits back in his chair with an air of approval. Of course St. Pascal is brimming with je ne sais quoi. We practically invented the phrase.

"If you have a moment, you should make the trip out to Diaz's Grand Illusions," I say, filling his glass once more. The table turns to me. I guess they're not used to penguins speaking, but I continue nonetheless. "It's a magic shop. It's filled with great stuff."

"Dr. Von Thurston won't have time to do that,"

Derek says. He lifts his glass for me to refill as well. "But I will. It's always good to check out the competition."

I note how Derek doesn't call him Dad. It's sort of what I have to do when I'm working at the hotel with my own dad. I make sure to call him Mr. Vance so I don't confuse anyone.

"We own at least ten magic shops around the world," Dr. Von Thurston explains. "We are never not within reach of a trick or two."

"Well, if you're interested in opening another shop, let's talk location," Mr. Maple says. "The Crossed Palms Resort would be the perfect spot for a new store."

Dr. Von Thurston addresses the woman with the feathered hat. "Talking business is such a cliché thing to do at a convention. Wouldn't you agree?" The lady laughs gaily while Mr. Maple bristles in his chair. I guess it must be hard for him not to be in command of things. After a long pause, Mr. Maple laughs so loudly it breaks the tension. Dr. Von Thurston joins him, and soon the whole table is cackling enough to disturb the poor guy onstage. Thankfully, that magician is finished with his speech and welcomes out another master of ceremonies.

"And now please join me in welcoming St. Pascal's

very own magical enchantress—the beguiling Angela, the Sorceress of Wonder!"

Guests erupt in applause. Angela looks radiant in a formfitting sequined gown. Everyone is *so* in for a treat. To start off her set, Angela does card tricks. Although card tricks are usually hard to follow in such a large ballroom, Angela manages to capture the room's attention with ease. She's quick-witted and funny, and she selects audience members to join her onstage.

"Now, who wants to be my next victim—I mean, *volunteer?*" she asks with a wink. The guests are a little nervous, but eventually a couple of people take Angela up on her offer.

As Angela continues with her show, I refresh Dr. Von Thurston's glass yet again. I don't get it. He's drunk so many glasses of iced tea but hasn't once left the table to use the restroom. He must have a strong bladder. Or this is all part of an elaborate magic trick. I'm kind of in awe.

Angela's next trick involves large silver rings. She's so graceful onstage, like a ballet dancer. I get so caught up watching her I fail to notice Derek raising his glass for me to refill. He's holding the glass so high it obscures my view.

"Sorry," I whisper, and replenish his drink.

"Can you direct me to where the restrooms are?"

Well, at least Derek isn't like his father. I ask him to follow me.

"The real trick in performing with the ol' linking rings is to make sure you don't make any noise when you link them," he says. "If you do, then you clearly have not been practicing."

"There you go." I point to the restrooms, but Derek is not done explaining the trick.

"And you have to find ways of directing where the audience should look. That's called a 'misdirection' in the biz—"

"Thanks for the tip, but I'm not into magic tricks," I finally interrupt. "My thing is detective work. I'm a detective. The Crossed Palms Resort's assistant house detective, in fact."

Derek raises his eyebrow.

"I find that hard to believe. It looks to me as if you're just serving drinks," he says. "Not many of the waitstaff are solving mysteries."

"Well, if you must know, I'm actually working undercover." This is technically not a lie. Even though I'm serving drinks, I *am* still working the room, scanning for anything out of the ordinary. "Besides, plenty of people are skilled in multiple ways. I can serve a drink while also noticing what color tie a man seated at the far end of the ballroom is wearing and how he wears one dangling earring on his left earlobe." I pause for effect. "It's purple-gray. The tie, that is. Take a look."

Derek has a few things to learn. The waitstaff are skilled workers. They have to anticipate needs way before a guest even has them. Some of them walk around in heels. I refuse to wear heels and instead wear my comfortable penny loafers with my tux.

"Working undercover? Really?" Derek asks with a lilt in his voice, implying he doesn't believe me. "What's your name?"

"Goldie. My name is Goldie Vance."

"Goldie?" There goes the lilt again.

I nod. "That's my name. Don't wear it out!"

"Well, Goldie Vance, unlike *you*, I'm an actual detective," Derek says. Then he pulls out another business card, as if I didn't already have one in my pocket from our conversation fifteen minutes ago.

"It says *part-time* detective," I remind him.

"That's correct. I am what you might call a

Renaissance man," he says. "I dabble in a lot of things. Magical arts. Mystery solving. I even write my own poetry. Let me recite my last poem. It's titled 'Ode to the Cantaloupe.'"

Before he finishes clearing his throat, I put a stop to his performance.

"I have to go back and serve more drinks, but thank you. I'll make sure to catch your poem next time."

I rush back to the table before Derek can open his mouth again. Boy oh boy! I had no idea I would spend tonight dodging poetry and explaining the importance of hospitality to a hotel guest, but here I am.

"Goldie, you're muttering to yourself," Cheryl says.

"Sorry, I didn't notice," I say. I need to pull myself together. Can't let Derek ruffle my feathers.

Angela performs the grand finale where she makes eight doves appear out of nowhere. She incorporates Antonio Vivaldi's *The Four Seasons* into the show to heighten the drama. The audience claps with glee as she produces one dove after another. Although I'm busy making sure everyone's glass is full, I'm glad I'm able to catch glimpses of the finale.

"Let's give another round of applause to Angela, the Sorceress of Wonder!"

Angela returns to the stage and takes one more bow. A guest hands her a large bouquet of roses, a much-deserved gift for such a wonderful act. I'm glad Angela's getting the recognition she deserves in front of her peers.

Mr. Maple now takes the mic.

"Welcome to Crossed Palms Resort, the hotel where everything is at your disposal. I am the owner of this establishment. You can call me Mr. Maple."

Well, duh. That *is* his name.

"Please join me in a toast," he says. The entire audience raises their glasses, which signals for Cheryl, Rob, and me to run around and do our job. We're speed racers, eyeing glassware like they're sparkling diamonds to take. Being a server is not a job for turtles.

Once all the guests' glasses are ready, Mr. Maple continues: "May you enjoy your magical oasis, and may your tricks stay within your mind and not in your wallet."

I think most people in the audience don't quite understand what Mr. Maple is saying, although they clink their glasses anyway. Oh, Mr. Maple. I guess not everyone is meant to captivate an audience on the stage like Angela.

I head to the kitchen and start handing out dinner plates. From that moment on, the night moves quickly. I don't have any more encounters with Derek. In between dinner and dessert, we're allowed to take a mini break, and I couldn't be happier. My feet are killing me. Rob, Cheryl, and I collapse outside the ballroom, plates in hand. Angela spots us and wanders over to chat.

"You were great, Angela," Cheryl exclaims before shoveling a big heap of lasagna into her mouth. "I love your doves so much."

"Thank you! Everyone seemed to enjoy it!" Angela says with a smile. "By any chance, have you seen any of my silver rings? I seem to have misplaced one of them."

"Not at all," we say in unison.

Angela shakes her head. "So strange. I'm sure it's here somewhere."

"After the party, we'll take a good look," I say. "Promise."

Soon enough, the bell rings and we're off to clear the plates. Before the rest of the guests can rush to vacate the ballroom, I see Dr. Von Thurston and Derek whisked through a side entrance.

What a night! I am officially wiped out.

"Darling Goldie."

I notice the familiar whisper-talk right away. Miss Dupart sits alone at a table, wearing a very glamorous floral dress and what seems like all her favorite pieces of jewelry. "Can you do me the honor of walking me back to my room? I must tend to my beloved Clementine."

"Sure thing, Miss Dupart. Clementine didn't want to be your date?"

"Clementine simply refused to make an appearance." She wraps her ringed fingers around my arm. I'm surprised to see Miss Dupart at this type of event. It's a bit late for both of us.

"Didn't take you for a lover of the magical arts, Miss Dupart."

"Oh, darling, I am well versed in the arts of illusion and mysticism," she whisper-talks. "When you've been an entertainer as long as I have, you must be skilled in many different mediums, if you will."

"That's funny! I was explaining that to someone earlier tonight," I say as we walk past the crowded lobby filled with magicians. "What do you think about Dr. Von Thurston? I met his son, and boy, he's quite something."

Miss Dupart pauses by the elevators. When an elevator arrives, we let a group of guests enter ahead of us and wait for the next one.

"I worked with Dr. Von Thurston briefly many, many years ago, long before the appearance of his son," she says. "He had this wonderful act out in the Catskills. I was his assistant back then, but I was too much of a presence for him. When I refused his requests to keep in the background, my assistant role went poof! Gone! Just like magic!"

I chuckle. I can't imagine Miss Dupart staying quiet for anyone, even Dr. Von Thurston. Miss Dupart is meant to be seen *and* heard.

"Rumor has it Von Thurston continues to mistreat his assistants and never acknowledges their hard work," she says, shaking her head. "Some men simply prefer bogarting the stage for themselves."

"I guess you're right, Miss Dupart. It's why I love Angela's show," I say. "She always finds a way of allowing the audience to participate. Her assistants are given their own time to shine, too."

Angela is too cool. When she's not doing performances like this, she shares the stage with two other female magicians. I really admire that about her. Who wants to enjoy the limelight by themselves? The more the merrier, I say.

We finally arrive in front of Miss Dupart's hotel room.

"I hope you enjoyed yourself, Miss Dupart," I say as I hold open the door for her.

"I always do," she says. "And now if you'll excuse me, I must strip away this costume and ask the stars to bless me with their potent power."

She pats my hands a couple of times, and I wait until she closes the door behind her. I like the idea of stars twinkling down on Miss Dupart as she slumbers away.

I finally grab hold of the bow tie around my neck and yank it off. Thank goodness I no longer have to wear *this* costume. Good-bye, strangling. Overall, my night dressed as a penguin went well. I didn't spill iced tea on anyone, not even Derek Von Thurston. If that isn't a magical feat of epic proportions, I don't know what is.

Now if only I had magic to transport me to my bedroom so I could hit the sack.

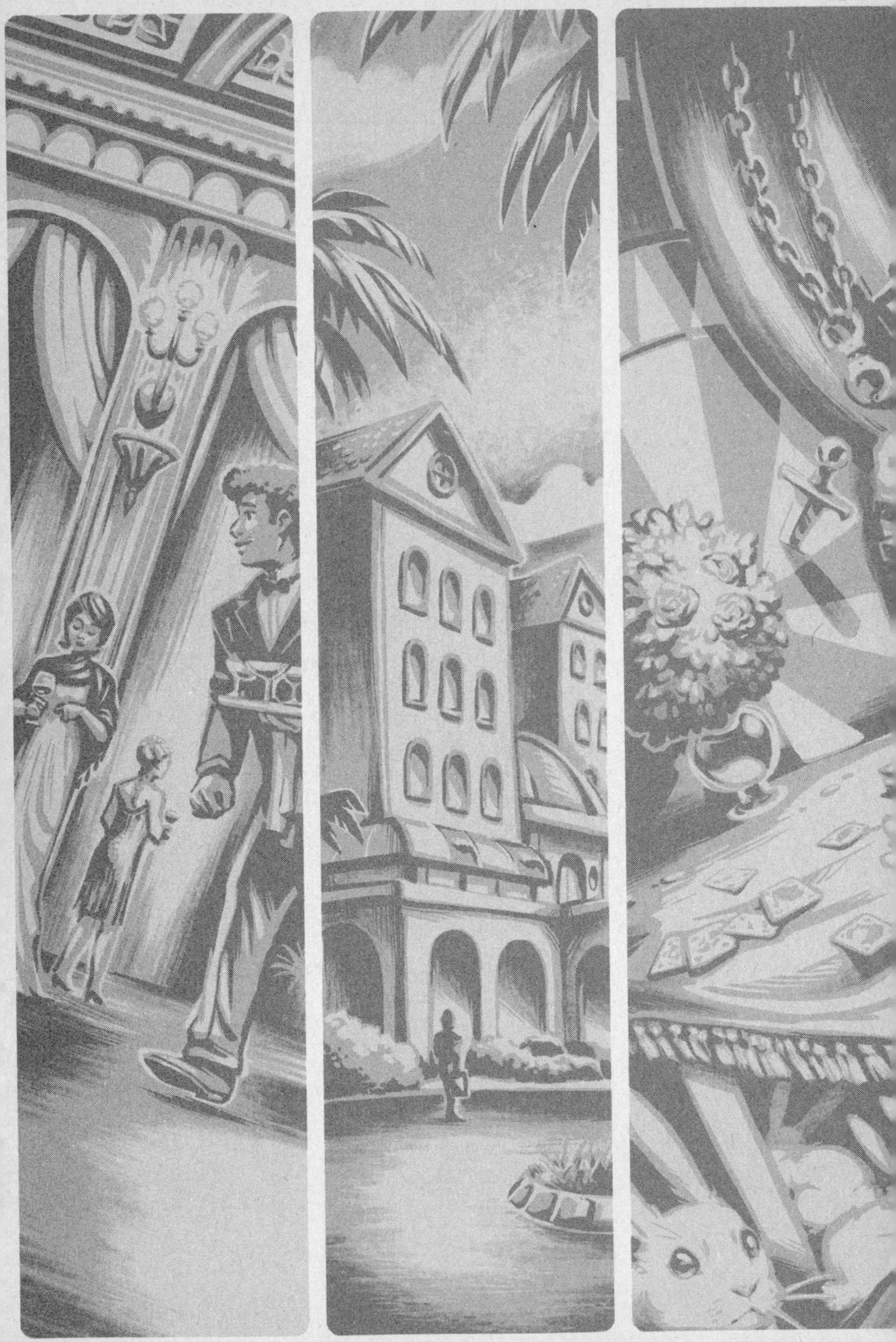

Chapter Five

MY FEET ARE THROBBING. THEY'RE PERFORMING THEIR own show, and it's a full-on Latin jazz percussion solo on the timbales. I bet I'm not the only one with drumming toes. Rob and Cheryl must be suffering as much as I am.

The one silver lining from working late last night is that today I don't have to! I'm so jazzed! I jump out of bed and greet Dad with a big hug.

"Good morning, Daddio!"

"Well, someone woke up on the right side of the bed." Dad sips his coffee.

"You bet I did! I don't work today, which means I get to have fun."

"Well, sunshine, you're one lucky person," Dad says as he gets up. "I, on the other hand, must clock in. Don't forget. You're still due at your mother's for breakfast."

Breakfast! My favorite meal of the day, especially when my mom's cooking it.

"Hey, Dad. Did Angela ever find her missing silver ring last night?" I ask.

Dad shakes his head. "I'm sure it will show up today." He gives me a kiss on the forehead before heading out. "Any big plans for your day off?"

"Date with Diane. The biggest plan ever!"

"That *is* a big plan! Enjoy your day, sunshine. I love you."

"Love you too, Dad."

I rush to get dressed and get ready to hop on my bike. Mom is just a brief ride away. Mom and Dad are no longer married, but it's not a big deal. We live close by, and when I'm not staying with Dad, I'm hanging with Mom over at her apartment.

Dad's house is located on the grounds of the Crossed Palms Resort, so I pop into the main hotel. Because it's so early, there's barely anyone up. I say hello to the front-desk workers and those tidying up the lobby. It's hard to imagine that the hotel was overrun by magicians just a few hours ago. It's so quiet now.

Then I pedal up Main Street and take a deep breath. The smell of jasmine permeates the air. Not a cloud in the sky. It's as if everyone and everything is aware of my date with Diane. Sure, last night was a bust, but that won't be the case tonight.

I spot the restaurant I'm taking Diane to: Josephine's. It's closed, of course, but soon I'll be seated out in the back somewhere with Diane, ordering French-sounding dishes. Would Diane want me to order for her? Hmmm. I don't think so. I'll let her decide.

Hold on. I hit my brakes. What was that on the door? I direct my bike to the entrance of the restaurant.

A sign affixed to the door reads in big bold letters: JOSEPHINE'S WILL BE CLOSED TONIGHT DUE TO AN UNEXPECTED PRIVATE EVENT. ALL RESERVATIONS WILL BE ACCOMMODATED AT A LATER DATE. SORRY FOR THE INCONVENIENCE.

"Noooooooo!"

What treachery is this? Who is to blame? Why are the stars conspiring against my date with Diane? What a complete bummer. But there's nothing I can do about it right this second. All I can do is punch it over to Mom's to figure out a plan B. Stat!

"Hey, babe! Is that you?"

I hear Mom from the kitchen. The smell of bacon wafting out is heavenly, but it's not enough to comfort me after this catastrophic change of plans.

"Mom! Josephine's is closed," I yell before collapsing onto the sofa.

"Well, of course it is. It's only eight o'clock in the morning. They don't open until later." Mom walks into the living room wearing a loose-fitting blue house-dress. Her hair is up in a ponytail.

"No, I mean it's closed *all day*, and I had reservations for tonight!"

Mom gives me a warm hug. "I'm sorry about that, babe. Is it a private event?" I nod. "It must be something big to have rented out the whole restaurant. It probably has to do with the magic convention, don't you think?" She leads me away from the sofa and to the kitchen table. "Eat up. I made your favorites."

Love really is bacon, eggs, and pancakes. "Thanks, Mom."

"I'm sure you'll find somewhere else to take Diane."

She's right. I can't keep fuming over Josephine's

closing. I'll come up with another fun plan. At least I hope I will.

"How did last night go?" Mom asks. "The Mermaid Club was open all night. Magicians sure love mermaids."

Mom works as a dancing mermaid at the always-popular Mermaid Club. She swims underwater for long periods of time, like a sea goddess.

"My feet still hurt from standing and serving endless pitchers of iced tea."

"I bet, babe."

"I also met this boy named Derek Von Thurston, the son of the great Dr. Von Thurston. Would you believe he gave me this card?" I pull out Derek's now-wrinkled business card and hand it to Mom.

"Part-time magician and part-time detective? You two must have so much in common."

I scrunch up my face.

"No?" she asks while pouring me a glass of orange juice. I'm so glad it's not iced tea. I don't think I'll ever drink a glass of iced tea for as long as I live.

"He's a bit of an explainer. He likes to have the answer for absolutely everything," I say. "It's a tiny bit annoying."

Mom sits down and cracks open a boiled egg. The sun's rays are blanketing the kitchen with a soft, luminous glow. Mornings here are enchanting.

"You might want to give Derek another try," she says. "He must travel all over the world with his father. It's probably hard for him to make new friends. And think about having to carve out time to be with your father when he's constantly working."

I hate to say it, but maybe Mom is right. Derek may like to yak it up, but maybe he's overcompensating. Mom and Dad both live very busy lives, but they always make sure I'm getting enough attention and love. It seemed like Dr. Von Thurston was constantly performing last night with his many stories and jokes. Perhaps Derek was just doing the same thing.

"I didn't think about that," I say.

"Now, I'm not saying you have to be best friends," Mom says. "Just try to understand where his actions may be stemming from."

Derek Von Thurston is a guest at the resort. I'll try my best to not shut him down so quickly.

"Better enjoy your breakfast. You'll need your fuel for today."

I do as she says. Adventure is just a bike ride away. I'll figure out somewhere else to take Diane.

"Thanks, Mom," I say. We eat while I tell her everything about Angela's dove performance.

A couple of hours later, I arrive back at the hotel. I lean my bike against the hotel wall, in a little nook that seems specially made for it. Unlike the emptiness and stillness of a couple of hours ago, the resort is brimming with action. The convention is in full swing today.

"Good morning, Cheryl!"

Cheryl also has the day off, but I'm not surprised to see her here. We always seem to gravitate to the places we love. Rob is around here somewhere. I'm sure of it.

"Hi, Goldie. I've got something for you." Cheryl's ditched her usual pink blazer for a snazzy teal summer dress. She walks behind the hotel's front desk and pulls out a badge with a picture of a top hat and a magic wand on it.

"What's this?" I ask.

"It's just a little something. Since we worked so hard last night, we're allowed to take as many magic workshops as we'd like. It's free access!"

Neato! *Free* is always a great word to hear.

"Hey, penguins! How's it waddling?" Rob asks.

Without missing a beat, Cheryl hands Rob a pass and a pamphlet.

I notice how the other hotel workers are eyeing us. That can mean only one thing: They're about to ask us to do some work, and we can't have that. It's time to take this meeting out of the hot zone.

"Let's get out of here before *you know what* happens." I give them a look, which is *our* look, not to be confused with any other looks. Now that I think about it, there are a lot of different looks to juggle. Thankfully, Cheryl and Rob get it.

We head over to the resort's cool atrium before someone can corner us. The atrium is located toward the back of the resort and is filled with beautiful, lush plants and flowers. It's a perfect place for us to talk and not be disturbed.

"What kind of workshops are we talking about?" I ask.

We each open up our own copy of the pamphlet and study the dense schedule. I had no idea the League of Magical Arts Convention would feature so many different workshops, seminars, and speakers. Not only is the Crossed Palms Resort host to a multitude of magic shows, both big and small, throughout the two-day convention, but there are also plenty of classes to perfect your spellbinding training.

"'Shuffle Set-up: Speed Dating for Magicians'?" Cheryl asks.

"'Flash Paper: Light Your Act on Fire'?" Rob suggests.

"'Abraca-Yoga'!" I yell.

Hundreds of different classes to choose from. It's amazing. How to be a great assistant. What the best wands are. A seminar on sleight-of-hand exercises. Mime exercises. How to work with animals. How to work with children. Even how to perform in a cape. It's a cornucopia of tricks.

"I'm interested in finding out what chemicals they use for the flashy tricks," Cheryl says. "What about you two?"

"I think I want to attend classes on how to be a better friend to a magician," Rob says. "Also, any workshop with Dr. Von Thurston's name attached to it."

I locate my pen and hand it over to Rob. He circles the classes he wants to take. Cheryl does the same. Then I get an idea.

"Do you think Diane would be interested in seeing a magic show with me?" I ask.

"What happened to Josephine's?" Cheryl asks.

"It's closed for a private event tonight," I say. I look back down at my pamphlet. "Hmmm, maybe I could take her to some magic workshops. What do you think?"

Cheryl and Rob both nod in agreement.

"With your pass, you're allowed to invite one guest. You could bring Diane along," Cheryl says. "I think it'd be a lot of fun!"

"A magic show," I say. "Like a real unexpected adventure."

I like this idea the more I think about it. Diane and I can explore the magical arts. It will be a new experience we can share.

"I think you two are right. I'm going to give her a call and ask," I say.

Cheryl comes up with another brilliant idea: We pick one class where we'll all meet so we can catch up. It takes a while for us to decide which class to choose. Cheryl finally finds the perfect one.

"Let's meet at 'Now You See Us, Now You Don't Soiree: A Get-Together for Assistants.'"

"Deal!"

We each circle the party, and our plans for our day off are set. I go to call Diane about the date while Rob and Cheryl head to their first workshop. Today is going to be a magical-wonderland kind of day, and I can't wait.

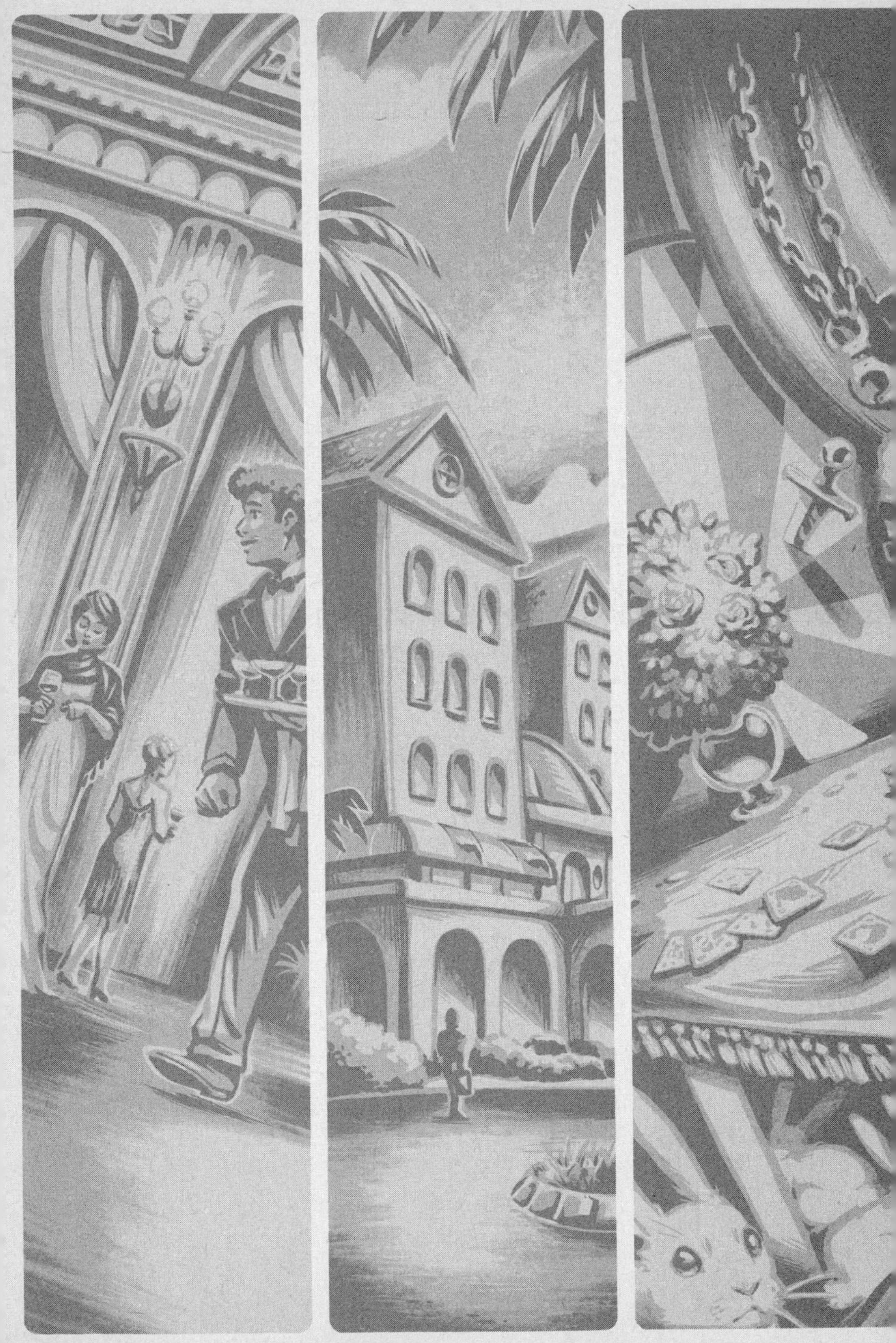

Chapter Six

THERE'S A BIT OF A LINE TO GET INTO THE ABRACA-yoga class. I knew it would be a popular one! I felt it in my bones, bones that will inevitably be bent and wrapped in a magical pretzel.

"Just one," I say to the woman at the check-in table.

"One pillow is available in the front row, if you want to scoot and take it," she says before checking my badge. "You can leave your shoes over there."

She points to a wall where shoes are lined up. All the chairs in the room have been replaced with large pillows. The curtains are drawn, adding a calm, cozy feeling to the room. After taking off my shoes, I plop down on a pillow between a woman toying with a piece of silk and a man jotting down notes in a leather-bound notebook.

"Abraca-yoga!" I exclaim, and they both laugh.

"Ganapati Socar is a renowned movement magician from India," the woman to my right explains. "He travels the world sharing his practice with so many. You're in for a treat."

"Movement magician?" I say. "I had no idea there were so many types of magicians."

The man beside me flips through his notebook and points to a page. "There are thousands of types! The goal is to stand out. You have to find your gimmick. What's yours?"

"Oh, I don't have a gimmick. I'm just a casual observer," I say. "A fan."

Ringing chimes alert us that the workshop is about to begin. Suddenly, the elevated stage becomes engulfed in fog. You can barely see a thing. I squint to get a view. It's no use.

"Namaste."

A voice from within the fog greets us. It's a very soothing voice, just the right tone. I'm already feeling relaxed. "Please repeat after me. Namaste."

Everyone in the room repeats the word, and as soon as we finish saying it, the fog lifts to reveal a young man dressed in a long bright-blue tunic with matching pants. He sits crisscrossed with no shoes. His eyes are rimmed with dark eyeliner and his thick black hair hits just below his shoulders.

"Welcome to abraca-yoga—a way not only to find enlightenment in the arts but also to expand the very limits of mind, body, and soul," he says. "To better attune ourselves to listening to these elements, let us begin with a five-minute meditation. Close your eyes."

I take a quick look around. Meditation is something I've tried a couple of times. I don't think it's really up my alley. My eyes are constantly in hawk mode, searching and checking for anything out of the ordinary. Still, I do my best. I shut my eyes tight and listen to Ganapati Socar guide us into a calm state of being, or something like that. Unfortunately, I can still hear the woman beside me fidgeting with the silk in the palm of her hand and the man beside me stowing his notepad away. Somewhere nearby a person coughs. Another moves. Trying to be quiet can be so loud.

"As you open your eyes, try to leave behind your worries," Ganapati says. "The following movements we'll be engaging in are meant to prepare us for the rest of the convention. Consider this a blessing to your limbs."

"My toes need extra blessings," I say. The man beside me shushes me.

Oops. I guess abraca-yoga means no yakking. Who knew?

Ganapati leads us into a couple of poses. Mountain pose. Warrior. Cobra. They're pretty easy to follow.

"Now that we've acquainted ourselves with the basic poses, make sure to incorporate them into your every day," he says. "We will now take abraca-yoga to the next level: communicating with your chakras through the use of the Chakra Cards."

"This is what he's known for," whispers the woman to my side.

"The Chakra Cards have been passed down from generation to generation." Ganapati paces back and forth on the small stage. "No one else has devised a way of incorporating the supernatural elements of being a magician with yoga, not only to supplement your life but also to empower you."

Ganapati sits crisscross again and closes his eyes. He rests his hands on his knees and mutters a couple of sayings I can't quite make out. The room is deathly quiet. Something is about to happen! I wait with anticipation. Suddenly, Ganapati begins to levitate.

Actually levitate. He floats just a few inches off the floor. I immediately want to get up and place my hand under to see how he's doing it. Is there a clear platform raising him up? I can't figure it out.

Ganapati eventually lowers back down to the stage, and I am in awe.

"How did you do it?" I shout. Those around me shush me. How can they not be asking the same question?

The abraca-yoga instructor smiles gently and walks over to where I'm sitting. I'll tell you this much: No matter how many mountain poses I do, I will never levitate. There's just no way.

"My child, you never divulge what is truly inside you. You just…do," he says. "Let us turn to the Chakra Cards and see what they have in store for each of us, including you."

Ganapati turns back to his stage. While he goes to retrieve his Chakra Cards, the rest of us drink water and loosen our bodies a bit. Walt appears at the door and I go to greet him. He's not dressed to do abraca-yoga, which is too bad. Walt could use some relaxing lessons.

"Good morning, Walt!" I say. "There's room in the front row if you want to join in on the Chakra Card–yoga pose stuff."

"Good morning, Goldie," he says. "Just making the rounds to see if any new information has come to light about the missing ring. Have anything to report?"

"Do I ever! Ganapati just floated above that stage for a full five minutes!" I say. "It's the living end!"

Walt presses his lips together. I guess it's not exactly what he's looking for. Oh yeah. Levitation is probably just par for the course at a magic convention.

"Sorry, Walt. Nothing to report."

Just when I finish saying that, we notice Ganapati wave hotel workers over. Walt and I join them backstage.

"They were right here," Ganapati says. His face is sweaty and flustered. "I don't understand where they would go. No one else was here. Not a soul. I touched them right before entering the stage. I pat them before each performance to reassure myself of their location. And now they are not here."

"I'm the house detective, Walter Tooey," Walt says.

"And I'm his assistant, Goldie Vance!" I pipe up.

"We'll figure this out together," Walt continues. "Let's scour this area before expanding the search."

Walt and I try locating the Chakra Cards with Ganapati. He says the deck has gold lamination that would make it stand out anywhere. It's also heavy because of the gold.

"Chakra Cards illustrate different energy points in the body. Throat, crown, third eye. Each card appears to each guest and reflects what they should be opening," he explains. "They are critical."

"Are you sure you didn't ask someone to hold them for you?" I ask.

Ganapati shakes his head. "I have my routine and I don't change it. Ever."

I believe him. Routine is everything. We look on the floor behind the few pieces of furniture located backstage. The room was stripped before the workshop, so there aren't that many places for cards to disappear. The crowd waiting for Ganapati to continue begins to get restless. Walt steps out and explains that we're dealing with some technical difficulties.

"Do you want to go over what happened one more time?" I ask, pulling out my pad.

Ganapati runs through his routine once again. "Before each performance, I sit and hold the Chakra Cards in my right hand. When the meditation is over, I stand and place the cards on my meditation table."

He points to a simple, low wooden table. I take a

closer look with my magnifying glass. There is a slight crack in the wood, barely noticeable. Something white is tucked in the crack. I pull it out—it's a piece of paper.

"Is this yours?" I ask.

Ganapati frowns and shakes his head.

"That's no ordinary paper. It's flash paper. I do not partake in flash paper. I don't believe in it," he says. "That is not mine, my child."

Ganapati sits down on his meditation table and cradles his head.

"My poor Chakra Cards. They are lost," he says. "So lost."

Walt tries to calm him down. "We'll do our best to locate the Chakra Cards. Do not lose hope, Mr. Socar."

The Chakra Cards seem to be irreplaceable, which means they are valuable. Stealing them means easy money for someone. I stare at the room full of emerging and experienced magicians.

"Where should we start the process? Do you want to close off the room and interview everyone before they leave?" I ask Walt.

He takes me to the side, away from the distraught Ganapati.

"No, no. Today is your day off," Walt says. "I'm more

than capable of handling a missing deck of cards. It'll show up somewhere."

"Walt! This is a mystery. I'm your assistant. You need my help."

Walt isn't budging. I know he means well, but I want to help.

"I'll manage this. You just try to enjoy your day." He pats me on my shoulder. I know he won't be changing his mind anytime soon.

I look over at Ganapati. Poor guy. All he wanted to do was open our chakras. Walt announces to the patiently waiting audience that the workshop is unfortunately cut short.

"We didn't even pull out our Chakra Cards!" shouts the woman in the front row. Others nod in solidarity.

I slip out the side door to avoid any more complaints about uneven chakras. If Walt says he can handle it, then I'm going to leave him to it. I look at my schedule. One item sticks out to me: "Flash Paper for Beginners." I don't know a thing about flash paper.

Walt insisted I continue enjoying my day. Well, my day now includes a workshop on flash paper. A little work and a little play can easily go hand in hand. I head toward Conference Room B.

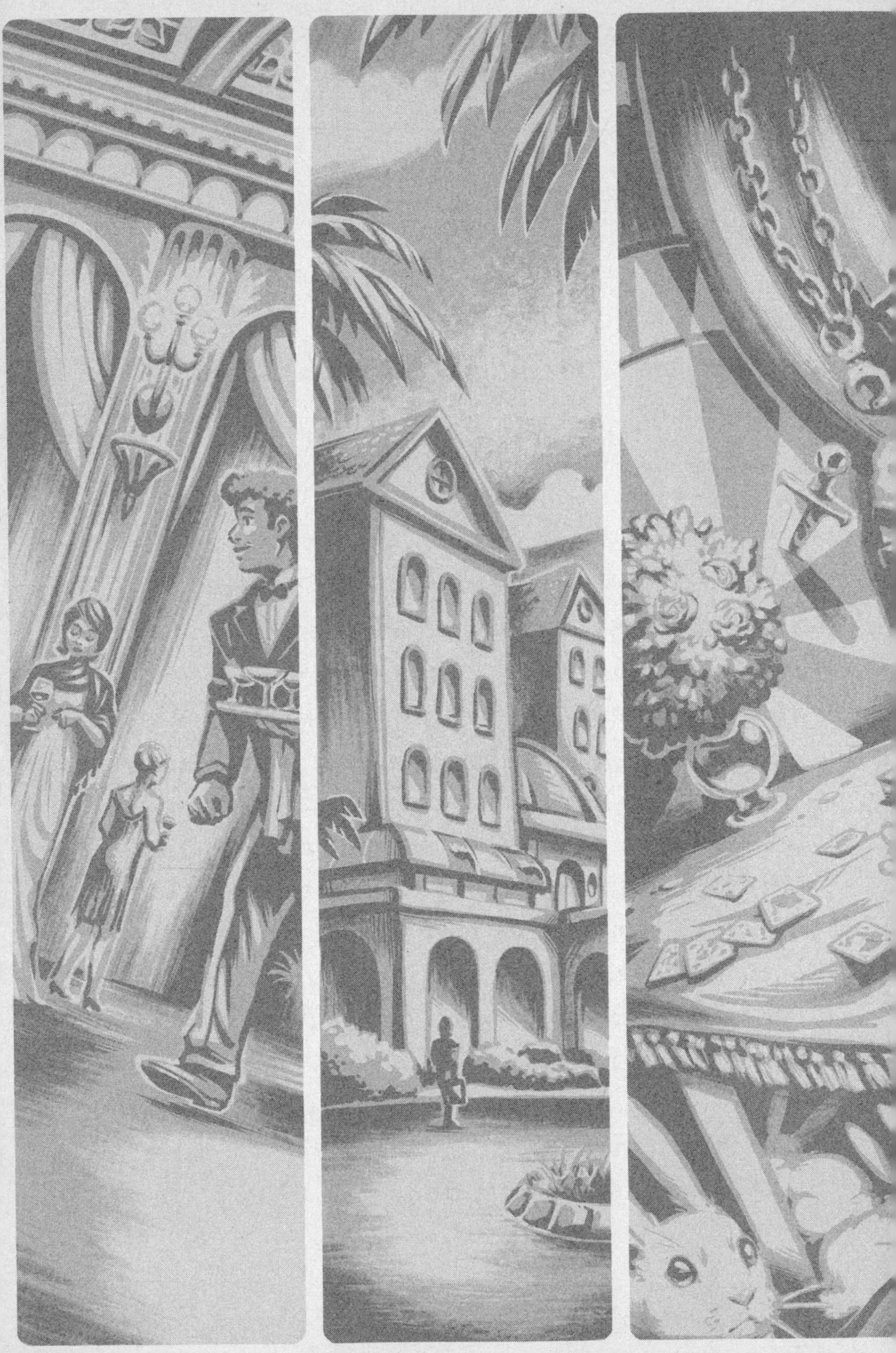

Chapter Seven

THE FLASH–PAPER–FOR–BEGINNERS CLASS IS NOT AS full as the previous workshop. Perhaps it's because flash paper is too technical and not mystical enough. If you asked me five minutes ago what flash paper was, I would have just said it was brightly colored paper, probably orange or red. Maybe with glitter on it. You know, something flashy! But now that the Chakra Cards are missing and all we can find is flash paper in their place, I know I need to find out more.

Crossed Palms Resort is such a big hotel. You can find a room for just about any meeting a guest might have. This particular workshop is being held in a small conference room. There are no pillows or even an elevated stage. Just regular ol' chairs and a small table. In front of the table stands an older gentleman wearing a very bright Hawaiian shirt. Unlike our previous instructor, he just waits for everyone to sit down. I guess he won't be making a grand entrance like Ganapati did, which is a total lost opportunity since he deals with fire.

The person I'm sitting next to is dressed completely in black with long black gloves, a tall black hat, and large dark sunglasses. The person on my other side is a young man who simply nods hello. I'm unable to sit in the front, but the conference room is so small that every seat has a perfect view. Once the last seat is taken, the instructor begins.

"I am Professor Blaze," he says. "I am the foremost authority in all things pyrotechnic. I've taught most of the great magicians how to utilize the power of fire to embellish their acts. If you want to add fire to your show, you come to me."

And with that, he tosses into the air an item that burns so brightly I have to cover my eyes. Professor Blaze is not kidding when it comes to fire. While he might have skipped a grand entrance, practically blinding the small, somber audience with a flash of fire is more than enough to wake us up.

"They don't call him Professor Blaze for nothing." I elbow the man next to me and he laughs.

"You want to make a bold statement? There's nothing bolder than using fire to add a little bit of fear and excitement to a performance," Professor Blaze says. "The utilization of pyrotechnics in a magical act is definitely not for the faint of heart."

Professor Blaze then proceeds to break down the history of magicians using fire in their shows. Apparently, it goes back to the very early magicians, when they would use candles for séances to call in the spirits. As magic shows became more and more elaborate and stepped away from intimate gatherings, the use of fire became somewhat of a norm. The bigger the show, the larger the pyrotechnics can be.

"You must not fall into the trap of using fire as a crutch," Professor Blaze warns. "Consider it more like a good accessory. It adds a bit of sparkle but should not make the whole outfit."

Like a good shoe or a yellow headband? I can follow that.

"Before we go blow things up, we have to start small," he says. "And by *small* I mean flash paper."

This is what I've been waiting for. If Professor Blaze is the expert in everything burning, then he'll be the right person to ask about the flash paper I found on Ganapati's meditation altar.

"Now, how many of you know what flash paper is?" he asks.

I raise my hand. "I just found out it is definitely *not* a very loudly colored piece of paper."

The audience erupts in laughter, as does Professor Blaze.

"That is correct. It's not just a piece of paper. It's a very important paper," he says. "Before I hand out pieces of flash paper, I want to go over its history."

Professor Blaze goes into serious-professor mode. I feel like I'm back in school, taking a history lesson from one of my teachers. The woman in black is paying close attention to Professor Blaze's lecture. As much as I want to be an attentive student, I can't help thinking about the missing Chakra Cards and what flash paper has to do with them. They must be connected.... But how?

"What if you want to burn something other than just paper?" the mysterious lady in black asks.

"Now, Mysteriousa, we've spoken about this before.

You just want to jump straight to the big show." Professor Blaze chuckles nervously. "You'll need to secure yourself permits. Not everyone is allowed to burn things. Safety is key. Safety not only for yourself but for your audience as well."

Mysteriousa! What a name. Unfortunately, the lady in black bristles beside me from Professor Blaze's answer.

"Burning tiny flash paper won't make much of a point, now will it?" she says.

Professor Blaze furrows his eyebrows.

"Mysteriousa, we all are very much aware of your show," he says. "You might want to tone down the want for bigger flames at more intimate affairs."

Mysteriousa scoffs, and I'm left with so many questions. What did Mysteriousa burn that cultivated her a reputation for it? Also, how does she feel about Chakra Cards? I grin at her before discreetly writing down her name alongside Professor Blaze's in my notebook.

"As I mentioned, flash paper should be used to add *flare* to your act. With that in mind, you should be thinking of how to light the paper," he says.

Professor Blaze pulls out a tiny, brilliant silver lighter. The lighter has his initials engraved in it.

"Say hello to Ms. Blaze. I don't go anywhere without her," Professor Blaze says. "This silver beauty has been a part of my act ever since my father gifted it to me on my tenth birthday."

The instructor twirls the lighter, flips it up in the air, and catches it behind him.

"You don't need a fancy lighter like mine. Any lighter will do, or even simple wooden matches. The trick is finding a way of igniting the flame without anyone noticing," he says. "And that takes practice. Sleight-of-hand practice. Plenty of workshops exist that will expand your sleight-of-hand work. I suggest daily exercises."

Professor Blaze manipulates his fingers, shuffling his lighter from one hand to the other until the lighter disappears completely. He does this so fast it's impossible to follow. If only I could slow down time to see what he's doing.

"Now, who wants to light some stuff?" he asks.

Finally. No more history lessons. Professor Blaze digs underneath the table and pulls out a wooden chest. It's small and, like his lighter, has an engraving of his initials.

"This here is my Chest of Flames," he says, patting the box.

"Is it important in the magician's world to give your props a special name?" I ask. I think it's a valid question. Professor Blaze pretty much has a nickname for every little thing.

"It can't hurt," he says. "These are your tools. They are part of your repertoire. It's always nice to add a little life to your objets d'art."

I'm all for cool nicknames. I mean, my name is Marigold, but everyone calls me Goldie. Perhaps my magnifying glass should also have a nickname, like Ms. Eyes or Mr. Oculus. I'll have to work on that. I jot the two possible names on a separate piece of paper in my pad.

The woman in black, Mysteriousa, raises her hand.

"Let's hold off on any more questions. Our time is slowly diminishing like a candle burning out," he says. "I want to be able to demonstrate the flash paper and give you each a hands-on experience."

Professor Blaze bursts a small flame from his palms. It's not as intense as before, but it's still very surprising. How he's able to turn his lighter on without showing it is a pretty cool trick. The audience and I clap.

"Okay, I'm ready to incinerate things," I say to my two seated colleagues.

"You can never be too ready," Mysteriousa says before adjusting the dark sunglasses that practically engulf her face. I wonder if I should wear sunglasses.

Professor Blaze opens the chest and starts to rummage through it.

"Um, one sec," he says.

The instructor slowly starts pulling items out of the chest. A top hat. A wand. Another hat. "They were right here."

He closes the chest, lifts it up, and looks underneath. I know exactly what's going on. Something is missing. Something important.

"One second," Professor Blaze repeats.

I excuse myself from my seat partners and join Professor Blaze at the front of the room.

"Professor Blaze, my name is Goldie Vance, and I'm the assistant house detective of the Crossed Palms Resort." Professor Blaze is much too busy trying to find his missing item to really pay attention to what

I'm saying. "What are you looking for? Maybe I can be of assistance?"

"It's the strangest thing. I placed them right here in this chest, like I always do," he says, scratching the back of his head. "I know I'm getting older, but I always place them in this chest."

Before I start the search, I have to ask the most important question: "What's gone missing, Professor Blaze?"

"My flash papers. All of them. Gone," he says. "Hundreds of flash papers. Just up in smoke."

Holy flaming papers!

"Are you sure you didn't leave them in your hotel room?" I ask.

Professor Blaze shakes his head. "I just arrived this morning, right on time for my workshop. My luggage is being held at the front desk. I haven't had a chance to go to my room yet."

Perhaps he forgot to pack the stack of flash papers, but Professor Blaze doesn't seem like the forgetting type. I still ask him. He shakes his head again.

"Is it okay if I take a look?" I ask.

I dig my hand into the chest. It's practically empty,

but I locate one piece of crumpled paper in the far corner. It was obscured by a Hawaiian shirt. I grab the crumpled paper and hold it up for Professor Blaze to see.

"Flash paper?"

He nods. I unfurl the paper and find a rabbit's foot hidden inside it.

"What in the world...," Professor Blaze says. "I've never seen that before in my life."

Now, I'm not one to believe in lucky rabbits' feet. They're a bit too gruesome, if you ask me. I say leave the rabbit and its tiny feet alone. But I'm hanging out with a bunch of magicians, and I'm not sure what the rules and rituals are.

"Are you sure this isn't your rabbit's foot?" I ask.

Professor Blaze shakes his head. "My thing is fire. I don't play with rabbits or kids or doves or anything breathing."

"Why would someone take your flash papers and leave behind a rabbit's foot?" I ask.

"Revenge!"

Mysteriousa has now joined the conversation. Professor Blaze doesn't seem too keen on having her be a part of it. Maybe it's because she's removed her sunglasses and her eyes are a bit ablaze when she says the word *revenge*! Dramatica is another name I would use for Mysteriousa.

"Now, now, Mysteriousa. You and I both know no one is envious of little old me," he says. "I'm practically retired."

Mysteriousa takes the rabbit's foot from my hand and holds it up to the light to inspect it, as if the foot will somehow tell us where the missing flash papers went.

"Magicians are all a bunch of envious, no-good, grandstanding, show-stealing thieves," Mysteriousa says. I'm surprised she didn't add a few cusswords, but I think she realizes I'm still a kid. Professor Blaze's face turns bright red from her angry outburst.

"Well, you seem to be part of this world," I say. "Got any clue who would steal flash papers from Professor Blaze?"

Mysteriousa adjusts her gloves and looks intensely at every single person in the audience. A deathly quiet blankets the room.

"We are all guilty for wanting to watch things burn. Every one of us," she says, pointing her finger at the audience.

"Calm down, dear."

Dear? Hold the flaming candlestick! Is Mysteri-ousa actually...

"This is my wife, and she's clearly upset over the missing flash papers," Professor Blaze says with an exasperated sigh.

Chapter Eight

MYSTERIOUSA CONTINUES TO DANGLE THE RABBIT'S foot for everyone to see until Professor Blaze calmly takes it away from her.

"Is it possible we forgot to pack the papers?" Professor Blaze asks.

Mysteriousa glares at him. "In how many years of teaching this workshop all over the world have you ever once forgotten a tool?" she asks. This time she calmly places her hand over his. "You are the most astute, observant, patient man I know. This is an act of *sabotage*."

Audience members gasp at the word.

"Now, hold on," he says. "Let's not go jumping to conclusions."

Maybe Mysteriousa is onto something.

"Who do you think would want to sabotage Professor Blaze's act?" I ask.

Mysteriousa takes off a glove and slaps it on the table. "Isn't it obvious? Richard the Talented, the Third Eye Association, the little girl who picked the wrong card, the valet boy from this morning who took our car keys and didn't hand us a ticket."

Professor Blaze gives me a resigned shrug. I recognize the shrug so well. I'm positive my father has done it plenty of times, when I go off on one of my tangents. I also can't help thinking about the valet boy. Thankfully, Rob is off today, so he couldn't possibly have made it onto Mysteriousa's long list of suspects.

"Anyone more specific?" I ask. "Perhaps someone attending the convention?"

Mysteriousa huffs with annoyance.

"Dear," Professor Blaze says to his wife. "It could be anyone."

Hmmm. Flash paper that's now a rabbit's foot…I need to bring this to Walt and the others.

Professor Blaze slowly closes the chest.

"I've never been one to add locks to my chest. I always have my important things near me." He draws Mysteriousa closer to him. She lets go of her angry demeanor and gives him a peck on the cheek. "My dear and this."

Professor Blaze pulls out his silver lighter, Ms. Blaze.

"The only other woman in his life," Mysteriousa says with a light laugh.

"Do you mind if I hold on to this?" I ask, pointing to the rabbit's foot. "I want to share my findings with Walt, the house detective. He'll want a full report from you both, if you don't mind."

Professor Blaze hands me the foot.

I pocket the evidence and say, "I'll be right back."

I run out and do a quick search of the hallway for Walt. Sadly, he's nowhere in sight. I rush over to the hotel lobby.

"Dad! I mean, Mr. Vance!" I yell. "Have you seen Walt? There are missing flash papers and I got this!"

I shove the rabbit's foot in Dad's face, startling him into taking two steps back. That's when I realize he's talking to a hotel guest. It's probably not a good thing to confuse the guests by dangling a rabbit's foot about.

"Excuse me, Goldie—let me introduce you to the Goldbergs," Dad says. "I'm showing them to the resort's restaurant."

I patiently wait for Dad to point them in the right direction. In the meantime, I take a closer look at the rabbit's foot. I pull out my magnifying glass (Mr. Oculus?). There's nothing out of the ordinary. No initials or indications of where the foot may have come from or who it may have belonged to.

"Shazam!"

I jump a bit, dropping the rabbit's foot. Rob!

"What's buzzin', cuzzin? Are you magically limber from abraca-yoga?" he asks. "I'm practicing being a magician's best friend."

How much of a friend can he be if he just scared the living daylights out of me?

"Hear me out, friend. I think something is going wrong with the classes," I say, picking up the rabbit's foot and showing it to him. "Have you seen Walt? I need to let him know."

Rob thinks for a second. He gestures across the lobby. "I actually saw him walking with Cheryl a second ago. They went that way."

"C'mon!" I grab his hand and we go running in search of them. Dad yells out to me, but I keep moving. No time to waste. When the scene of a crime is hot, you have to move quickly to gather as much information as possible.

Cheryl and Walt are quietly strolling outside, deep in conversation.

"Walt!" Rob yells, which causes them both to jump. I don't know what exactly Rob learned at "How to Be a Magician's Friend," but it must entail how to frighten people.

"Hey, what's the big commotion?" Cheryl asks.

"Missing flash papers and this," I say, once again brandishing the rabbit's foot.

Cheryl wrinkles her nose at the sight of it. "What are you doing with that?"

"At the flash-paper-for-beginners workshop, the flash papers went poof, and in their place I found this rabbit's foot," I say. Walt immediately starts to get nervous.

"Missing?" he says, and I nod. "First the Chakra Cards and now flash papers. Hmmm. You better take me to the workshop."

We quickly head back to the conference room, where Mysteriousa and Professor Blaze are seated in the now-empty front row.

"Hello, I'm Walter Tooey, the Crossed Palms Resort house detective," Walt says. "Goldie told me something has gone missing. Would you like to walk me through it?"

Cheryl, Rob, and I give Walt and the magicians privacy so that Walt can conduct his detective business. Whenever you're interviewing someone at the scene of the crime, you want to be free of any distractions. You also have to be an excellent listener and observer of body language. Right now Mysteriousa is gripping her black gloves with one hand and pointing to the chest with the other while Professor Blaze nods in agreement.

"Anything go wrong at your workshops?" I ask.

"Not that I could tell," Cheryl says. "Then again, the workshop I attended focused on the history of science in magic."

Rob sits at a table and we join him. "This could just be a coincidence."

I stare into Rob's big eyes. "One incident is a fluke, but two?" I emphasize my point by holding up two fingers.

"It's not as if flash paper is all that expensive or even useful, unless you're a magician," Rob argues.

"*Exactly*. That's what *proves* this is sabotage!" I insist.

"Goldie is right. This could be a problem," Cheryl says. "A big problem."

Glad to hear Cheryl understands the gravity of the situation. We glance over at Professor Blaze and Mysteriousa, who is being extremely animated in her expressions. I wonder if she's reached the part where she explains who the culprit may be.

After a few more minutes, Walt and the magic couple stand. Mysteriousa still has her scowl, which makes Rob a little nervous. When she walks over to me, she smiles.

"Walt has assured me you are both on the case," Mysteriousa says. "Professor Blaze, Ms. Blaze, and I are very happy you're taking this seriously. We hope you'll find answers quickly."

I am liking Mysteriousa more and more.

"Are you house detectives, too?" Professor Blaze asks. Cheryl and Rob shake their heads.

"But we *do* work at the hotel and are at your service," Rob says.

"Don't trust anyone!" Mysteriousa stares intensely at each of us.

"Let's get going, dear. I have to hunt for more flash papers before my next workshop begins," Professor Blaze says.

"I've got the perfect solution," I say. "Diaz's Grand Illusions. It's St. Pascal's very own magic shop. You can't miss it!"

I give them directions to the shop. Grand Illusions will have flash papers and more. "Just tell Mr. Diaz I sent you!"

"Goldie's right. You can't go wrong with Grand Illusions," Rob adds.

"Thank you so much! You are all true magicians' friends," Professor Blaze says before leading Mysteriousa out of the room by the arm. Walt shuts the door behind them.

"We've got ourselves a bona fide mystery, don't we, Walt?" I'm eager to get on the case. I've already filled my pad with pages of notes—more than enough to start the ball rolling.

Walt holds both his hands up.

"Let's not jump to conclusions. I want the three of you to continue to be vigilant," he says. "No need to worry the conference guests right now. All we have are a rabbit's foot and a piece of flash paper. Not quite enough clues to go on."

Not enough clues? What in the world is Walt talking about? I think those two clues are more than enough to have us question the other magicians.

"I don't know, Walt. I think the time to act is now. Cheryl can give us a list of the attendees who signed up for the workshops."

Cheryl looks down at her clipboard. "That would be a problem. The workshops are open to anyone with a badge, just like you. Guests can come and go whenever they want," she says. "No one is tallying up who is attending the classes."

This is a problem I didn't quite take into consideration.

"How about we round up all the instructors and—"

Walt shakes his head so roughly I'm afraid it might pop off.

"No, no, no. We are not rounding up anyone. Your job is to continue paying attention to what is happening. All of you. Eyes open."

Eyes open indeed. I pull out my magnifying glass. "Do any of you want to borrow Mr. Oculus?" I ask. Rob and Cheryl look confused, as does Walt, but I'm used to Walt's confused or exasperated face.

"Mr. Oculus?" he asks.

"Yes. I've decided to christen my important tools with nicknames. They are—what did Professor Blaze call them?" I rub my forehead, trying to remember what he said. "Oh yeah, objets d'art! That's French, you know!"

95

Walt cradles his head with his hands.

"Do you think I should come up with a nickname?" Rob asks. "Maybe that's something that would be kind of cool to mention to Dr. Von Thurston when I finally meet him. What do you think?"

As if on cue, the boy I've been successfully avoiding this morning pokes his head into the room.

"Good morning!" Derek Von Thurston says.

Instead of a blue velvet suit, Derek wears a completely yellow outfit: yellow short-sleeved button-down shirt, yellow slacks, and matching yellow jacket. His threads are quite something, not that I'm passing judgment. If looking like a sun is what Derek wants, I'm sure the sunflowers are happy.

"I just caught Professor Blaze before his workshop ended. He and my father go way back," Derek says. He already has his card in his hand, as if anyone asked for it. "Professor Blaze taught me how to light my first fire. He's a dear friend. He mentioned something about a theft."

He hands Walt his card. "I can be of service."

Now it's my turn to interrupt. Derek can't possibly be thinking he's going to help on this case. This is my case. Plus, Walt doesn't even think there *is* a case, so Derek's point is moot either way.

"That's a great idea. Do you think your father might be joining us, too?" Rob says, peering over Derek's shoulder just in case Dr. Von Thurston is near.

"Another workshop is about to begin here. We need to head out." Walt nudges us to exit the room. It's his polite way of avoiding Derek's question. Misdirection may be a magician's skill, but Walt is a pro at it, too.

"Thank you for your offer. We're on it," Walt says. "And now if you'll excuse me. Goldie, mind what we talked about earlier."

Walt hurries along. Too bad Derek doesn't hurry along with him.

"I see you got some notes. I've got notes of my own," Derek says, pulling out a notepad identical to mine from inside his yellow jacket. "A true detective always takes thorough notes. Did you take a statement from Professor Blaze and Mysteriousa? Mysteriousa already named suspects."

Cheryl raises her eyebrows. She knows exactly how I feel without me even saying a word. She knows Derek is a bit too much. Way too pushy.

Rob, on the other hand, is too enchanted to see what is right before his eyes.

"Like Walt said, we've got this under control," I say. "You should be doing what you're meant to be doing here. Greeting fans and performing tricks. Right?"

"What I'm meant to do here is solve mysteries. It's sort of like being a doctor—you go where you're most needed," he says. "Where do you want to exchange notes? Here or over by the breakfast buffet?"

Cheryl and I start to walk away, but Derek—and Rob, for that matter—are hot on our heels.

"There's a definite connection between the flash papers and the missing Chakra Cards," Derek says. "My guess is it's a plot by a nefarious group of magicians hungry for fame."

I stop in my tracks. "How do you know about the missing Chakra Cards?"

Derek smugly smiles. "A good magician never reveals his source."

I tilt my head. Is that how the saying goes? I don't think so. There's no way Derek is going to be a part of this case. I don't care how many business cards he hands out.

"Listen, Derek, you need to allow the professionals—i.e., me and Walt—to handle the missing cards and papers," I say. "Now, if you'll excuse me, my associates and I have a lot to discuss."

Derek bristles, but he's not deterred. In fact, I think my declaration only makes him more determined to join us.

"Interesting reaction. Would I be too forward in thinking that perhaps you are hiding something?" he asks. "Where were you this morning when Ganapati began his workshop?"

Cut the gas! Is he actually trying to interrogate *me*?

"We better head to the next workshop," Cheryl says, looking wearily at Derek, then at me. "Good luck, Goldie. I'll see you both at the rendezvous."

"Rendezvous?" Derek says. "Where's that?"

I can't help pulling a "Walt" and smacking my forehead.

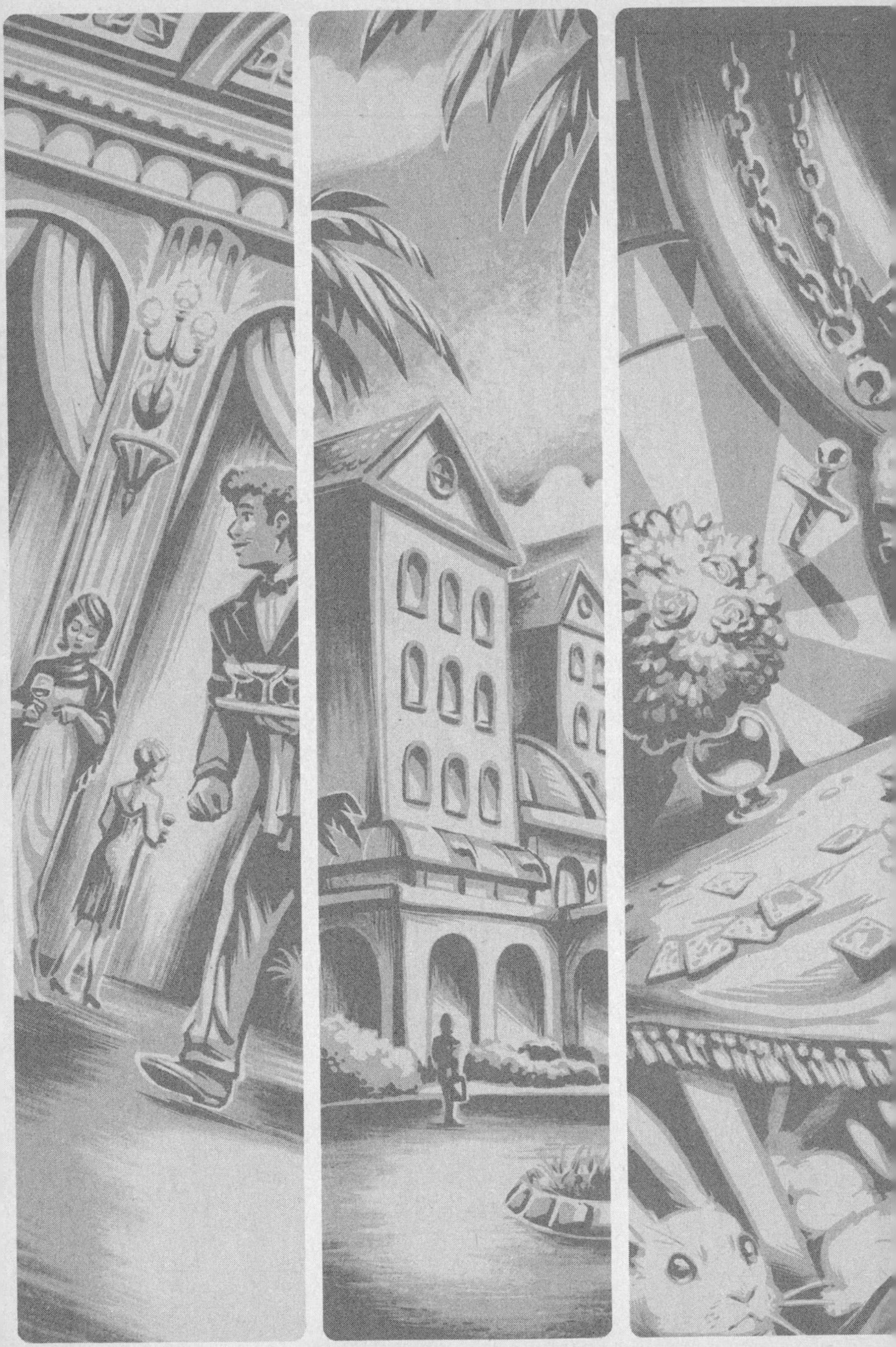

Chapter Nine

ROB PATS DEREK ON THE BACK. "I'LL CLUE YOU IN. NO sweat."

I give Rob an icy glare. He's so infatuated by Derek and the Von Thurston legacy that I can't rely on him to read any of my signs. I get it. I would probably be the same way if a great detective were among us. But now is not the time to lose focus. When Cheryl started working at the hotel, we became inseparable. Cheryl practically ended my sentences for me. Rob didn't join us until a little later, but when he did, we became the Three Musketeers. Now it feels like Rob is trying to convert our trio into a quartet.

"What's your father doing right now?" Rob asks. He rubs his belly. He must still be walking around with the Dr. Von Thurston book hidden under his shirt.

"He's busy preparing for his big show tomorrow," Derek says. "There's meditation, a massage, and a private mime class."

Although part of me wants to ask him about the mime class and how it plays into his father's act, I bite my tongue. "Did *you* attend any workshops today?" I ask instead.

"A true detective would have asked that ages ago," Derek says with a smug look on his face. "No. My father and I were both at the breakfast bar this morning. I enjoyed the eggs Benedict and bacon."

"Great! Then you are both off my list." *For now*, I add silently.

"Who should we be interviewing next, Goldie?" Rob asks, anticipating Derek's next question, which I can tell is right at the tip of his tongue.

"Sorry, I've got other plans." Before Derek can say a word, I do a quick about-face and head to the elevators. "I'm going home. Later, alligators!"

"But your home is that way!" Rob yells, pointing outside. I pretend not to hear. There's so much to do before my date with Diane, and I can cover a lot more ground without Mr. Let Me Explain It All by my side.

Saying I'm going home is just a ruse. I don't

actually live in the hotel proper, but of course Derek doesn't know that. I reach the service elevator. Only certain hotel employees have access to this elevator. You need a special key for it to work. My dad has access. Cheryl, too, for emergency purposes only. Walt and Mr. Maple have access. And one other person. You guessed it—little ol' me!

I watch the service-elevator door close before Derek and Rob reach me. I need to speak to the custodial manager of the hotel. Alone. I press the button marked *B* for basement.

The Crossed Palms Resort has many tunnels, corridors, and underground hideaways. I've spent countless hours playing hide-and-seek on these grounds, so I'm familiar with most of the little nooks and crannies. But even I haven't explored every single place. There is one man who has: Mr. Yahontov.

Oh, how could I forget! Sometimes Mr. Yahontov has access to the service elevator, too. He usually gets the key from Mr. Maple or Walt.

Mr. Yahontov is in charge of the custodial-arts department at the hotel. Every day, from his office in the basement, he deploys hundreds of custodial workers throughout the hotel. The workers take to the guest rooms and conference rooms to make sure they are immaculate by the time the next group of people rolls in.

To achieve such an undertaking, you need someone really good at coordinating schedules. Since the League of Magical Arts Convention has so many workshops, you'd need a super-large schedule to get the rooms clean.

"*Zdravstvuyte!*" I say. That's hello in Russian. "How's the cleaning game?"

"No cleaning here, my lovely Goldie. Just a lot of work." He pulls a bandanna from his back pocket and gently wipes the sweat from his forehead. "What are you doing down below? Don't you have the day off?"

"A good detective never rests," I say. "By any chance, have any of your workers found gold cards in one of the conference rooms? They're called Chakra Cards, and they've gone missing."

Mr. Yahontov shakes his head. "I have heard about the situation and the answer is no. No cards and no missing papers."

Of course, Walt must have spoken to Mr. Yahontov and asked him to pay attention for any missing items. But Walt might have forgotten to ask this:

"Who set up the workshop rooms?"

Mr. Yahontov pulls out a large leather-bound book. He likes to call it his bible. With it, he knows exactly where everyone is meant to be and when. He's just like Cheryl in that way. A wiz at schedules, maps, and coordination.

"That is an easy answer. The only two people who set up those rooms are Melina and George," he says, pointing to the two names in his ledger. "They worked that floor. A total of five rooms."

Melina and George are some of our top workers. If they saw anything out of the ordinary, they would have immediately told Mr. Yahontov.

"And they didn't see a thing, huh?" I ask, just to make sure.

"Not a thing."

I catch the time on Mr. Yahontov's watch. Oh boy. I better hurry. I'm supposed to meet Diane in the lobby for our date in a little under half an hour. During the afternoon sessions of the convention, various magic shows will be popping up all over the hotel. I thought it would be fun for Diane and me to check them out. Little did I know I would also be working. I won't tell Diane. I'm not sure how she'd feel about our first date turning into a mystery, but it can't hurt to make sure the magic shows go off without a hitch.

"Mr. Yahontov, thank you so much for being so helpful," I say.

"Did I even help?" he asks.

"You sure did!" I say, and give him a quick hug.

Even if I didn't get any closer to solving the mystery, it's always nice to spend time with Mr. Yahontov in his basement of wonder.

I head back upstairs. Before exiting the elevator, I take a quick glance to make sure Derek is nowhere in sight. I go outside to the small cottage tucked a bit away from the hotel. Our lovely little home. It's small and perfect for Dad and me.

He's not home right now. Dad's probably trying to quell some "fire" at the hotel. I meander into the kitchen to make myself a peanut butter and jelly sandwich and then scarf it down with a tall glass of orange juice. Even though my mind is racing with images of floating magicians and Chakra Cards, I try to turn it off for just a second. Diane will be at the Crossed Palms Resort soon. Time to think about that instead!

I take off my yellow headband and open my dresser drawer. Numerous other neatly folded yellow headbands stare back at me. Which one should I select? I know. I'll wear the one I wore when I met Diane. It's seen so much, like the first day Diane glanced my way and smiled. One look and I was on the hook.

Now for the real question: Do I wear my blue capri pants or my *other* blue capri pants? It's a tough call. I want to look cute but not too dressed up. I need comfort but can't look as if I've been working all day. I stare at my closet, where a rack of capri pants hang. So many options.

"Talk to me, capris. Which one of you should I wear?"

I run my fingers over a few pairs of pants and then stop. This pair is calling to me. I make the obvious choice and pick the capris that make me happy. (Truth be told, all capris make me happy. They're the best! They let my ankles breathe, they have pockets for all my important tools—including Mr. Oculus—and they're so dang comfortable.) I change into my chosen outfit—a short-sleeved blue button-up and a yellow-and-pink striped sweater-vest. Done.

I hope Diane will like the magic shows. Afterward, we can meet Cheryl and Rob at the rendezvous. That should be fun! Right?

Okay, why am I doubting myself? I guess I'm nervous. Me? Nervous? When did that happen?

"Goldie Vance! Pull yourself together. Today is going to be a great day. And neither Derek nor missing Chakra Cards nor flash papers are going to ruin it," I say to myself. "Let's go!"

Everyone can use a pep talk. Sometimes you have to just give yourself one. I slip my comfortable loafers on and head out the door. The butterflies in my stomach are flying out of control. This happens every time I see Diane. Mom says it's just nerves and that I should harness the bubbles. *Think of it as an energy source. Excitement for the day*, she says.

Bubble energy!

THE LOBBY IS CROWDED WITH MAGICIANS. THANK-fully, Derek is nowhere to be found. Then again, neither is Diane. I hope she didn't change her mind or decide that magic is silly and a waste of time. Oh boy. What if that's the case and she's a no-show? What time is it?

"Goldie!"

There she is! She's wearing a black-and-white

striped T-shirt tucked into black slacks, and she has a yellow bandanna around her neck, adding just the perfect flash of color to her outfit. Her baby hairs make a very cute curl on the side of her face.

"You made it," I say.

"Hi, Goldie! I'm excited to see some magic. Aren't you?" Her shoulder bumps into mine, and I'm positive my butterflies do a twirl or two.

"I am. The schedule's chock-full of options," I say, pulling out the pamphlet for her to see. "Because it's such a beautiful day, I thought it would be nice to catch a show being held in the garden. What do you think?"

Diane smiles her magnificent smile. I've made the right choice!

"Do you want anything to drink? Maybe a glass of lemonade?" The hotel lobby always has drinks to keep the guests hydrated. I walk Diane over to the station to find Evan replenishing one of the pitchers.

"Hi, Evan! Do you mind if I pour some lemonade?" I ask, grabbing glasses for Diane and me.

"Sure thing," Evan says. "What's the word from the bird?"

"Just going to check out some magic shows with Diane." I introduce them.

"Nice to meet you, Diane. I hope you don't fall for this hocus-pocus like most people here," Evan says. "Nothing is more boring than performers trying to outdo each other."

I guess Evan is still annoyed with the magicians.

"I love all things mysterious," Diane says. "It's neat trying to figure out how they do it."

Did Diane say she likes mysteries? My heart skips a beat or two.

"The only mystery is seeing how the magicians' assistants do all the hard work," Evan says. "See you around, Goldie. Nice to meet you, Diane."

I hand Diane a glass of lemonade. She clinks her glass against mine before taking a sip. I should have made a toast. Next time for sure.

"Shall we?" I say. Diane nods, placing her empty glass on the table next to mine, and we make our way through the crowded lobby toward the garden.

I was right. The weather *is* beautiful. Not a cloud in the sky. It's not too hot or too cold. Just a sweet breeze stirring the air.

Out in the garden, the hotel has set up a space with chairs for the audience and a short stage for the magician to perform on. Because I want to see the action, I lead Diane to the front row. That way I can spot if anything goes wrong.

"Do you know any magic tricks?" I ask.

Diane shakes her head. "Not really. Truth be told, I've never been to a magic show before. This is my first."

Is it weird I feel all kinds of pressure now? If this magic show doesn't deliver the goods, will Diane be disappointed in me? I need to put the kibosh on this thinking. Our date just started and I need to cool it. This is an adventure.

"A butterfly is saying hello to us." Diane points to the beautiful monarch butterfly flying above us. "Maybe she wants to enjoy the show, too." Now, that's a good sign if ever there was one!

A magician wearing coattails and a top hat takes the stage. He's a regular ol' penguin, just like I was last night.

"Esteemed guests! You are right where you belong!" he says with a very cute British accent. "My name is Sir Thomas Browne, but my friends call me Sir Thomas Browne. That's right. Get my name right, I tell them. I am here to astound you, perplex you, confuse you, and ultimately, hopefully, make you smile. Are you ready?"

The crowd timidly says yes.

"Hold on a second. My question to you was, *Are you ready?*"

This time we all scream a big affirmation. Our "yes" is so loud that Diane and I practically bust a gut.

Stop the presses! I see *him.* Derek is walking over to the front row. I want to play dead, but he's eyeing the empty seat right next to me, and there's nothing I can do about it.

Chapter Ten

"BEEN LOOKING ALL OVER FOR YOU," DEREK SAYS. I know I shouldn't, but I can't help rolling my eyes. Why is Derek pestering me? I'm right in the middle of my date with Diane!

"Shhhhh." I flash him the universal sign for quiet. It only makes him lean closer to ask me a question.

"I had a very interesting conversation with a"—Derek flips open his notepad—"a Mr. Yahontov. Do you know him? It was a little tricky to get to him, but I was able to persuade a housekeeper with his service-elevator key to let me ride down in exchange for a signed photograph of Dr. Von Thurston."

Do I know him? What kind of question is that? Derek is a shadow I never wanted, sort of like an annoying brother.

"Hi. My name is Diane." Diane sticks out her hand for Derek to shake. She says this in a whisper-talk, just like Miss Dupart would do. This makes me feel bad. I didn't introduce them and that was rude, even if Derek is annoying.

"Sorry about that, Diane—" Before I can do a proper introduction, Derek hands Diane a business card. She takes the card and smiles.

Sir Thomas Browne starts his first trick. It's hard to concentrate, what with Derek insisting on talking about Mr. Yahontov and his findings, which are identical to my own. We're both no closer to solving this mystery. Although, again, there is no mystery according to Walt. Not yet anyway.

"How do you two know each other?" Diane asks.

"We don't know each other," I say. "He's a guest. A Crossed Palms Resort guest."

Diane raises her eyebrow at my too-quick explanation. I hope she doesn't think I'm trying to cover something up.

"Well, Diana, it's a pretty simple story," Derek says.

"Her name is Diane, not Diana."

Derek clears his throat and starts over. "Well, Diane, as I was saying, it's very simple," he goes on.

"We are both on a case together. I'm calling it the Case of the Missing Props. I at first thought of naming it the Case of the Sticky Fingers, but thought that would be too obvious."

I find myself shrinking more and more into my chair. Diane is completely confused. I can't explain it right now, not when there's a show happening in front of us. Sir Thomas Browne is about to begin a trick involving cups and balls. The magician invites a man to join him onstage.

"This is an ancient trick, going back to the Egyptians. If you've visited Egypt, then you have surely seen this very same trick etched on a tomb like an informational illustration," Sir Thomas Browne says. "You doubt me! You shouldn't. These very fingers traced the ancient sketch. I've seen it all."

He rubs his forehead and says, "Well, my third eye has seen it all."

Diane and I giggle at Sir Thomas Browne's revelation. I could use a third eye to watch my surroundings while I roll my own eyes at Derek, who is scoffing at the magician's fanciful declaration.

"It's true. I'm a time traveler, and like these mystical red spheres I will ask you to pay close attention to, we will be traveling through space and time," Sir Thomas Browne says.

"I only ask that you don't lose sight of them. Or me," he adds with a wink.

While Sir Thomas Browne recites a very imaginative tale involving being stuck in the Sahara Desert with only one glass of water, the red balls disappear and reappear in the three copper cups before him. The man he selected from the audience is unable to follow exactly where the balls land. The crowd is mystified, as am I.

Derek skips to another page in his notepad and leans over to me.

"I heard the Sorceress of Wonder is missing a silver ring," he says. "Coincidence? I think not."

Yowza. How did I miss such an important clue? Angela's ring is still missing from last night's performance. As Walt once told me, there are no coincidences in our line of business. I can't believe Derek made that connection before me. Is it possible my sleuthing skills are slipping? No, I can't allow Derek to ponder this thought for even one second.

"Of course I know about the missing silver ring," I say. "It's on the top of my checklist."

"Did you interview the Sorceress? Because she revealed some interesting things to me," Derek says.

As I wait with bated breath for him to share what Angela said, Derek places his notepad back in his yellow shirt pocket. Unbelievable. He's not going to tell me, is he? Fine. I don't need his help. Or do I? I try my best to concentrate on Sir Thomas Browne. Anger can really cloud a person's focus.

"Is everything all right?" Diane whispers in my ear. "You seem distracted. Do you want to leave?"

Oh no. This is not how our date was supposed to go. I need to turn this attitude around. Not only am I with Diane but I'm also a great detective! If Derek wants to withhold important insight into the Case of the Missing Props, then so be it. As much as I want Derek to put a lid on it, he will not ruin my day.

"Nope. I'm having a great time," I say. "Look, Sir Thomas Browne is on to his next trick."

Diane wraps her arm around mine and I sort of melt. Forget about what Sir Thomas Browne is doing on that tiny stage. Enchantment is sitting right beside me.

After the cup-and-ball trick, Sir Thomas Browne thanks the audience member, who sits back in his seat.

The magician's next trick involves coins and a fishbowl. This time a young woman in a pretty, floral dress joins Sir Thomas Browne on the stage.

"Now, if you don't mind just sitting right here. You don't have to do a thing—just hold this empty fishbowl," Sir Thomas Browne says. The woman immediately starts laughing uncontrollably. I think the British accent is getting to her. Also, her nerves. I understand the feeling.

"I'm sorry!" the woman in the floral dress says as she tries to compose herself. "I can't help myself."

"Some people have said they can never take me seriously, but I didn't know how far this sentiment went until now," Sir Thomas Browne jokes, which leads the woman to have another laughing fit. The funny thing is when someone starts busting a gut like that, it often becomes contagious. Everyone in the small crowd begins to laugh along with her, including Diane and me. But not Derek. He's employing hawk eyes instead, staring intensely at the stage. I wonder if Derek ever relaxes.

"Are you missing something?" I ask. "Like a sense of humor?"

Derek shakes his head.

"I've seen this trick countless times. The old silver-coin trick," he says. "My father is far better at it."

I wonder what it's like to grow up with a magician and always be so aware of tricks instead of just enjoying them. Every time Sir Thomas Browne finds another silver coin behind the laughing woman's ear and drops it into the fishbowl, I smile. I guess I was sort of like Derek when I first saw his father's TV show, back when I was a kid. I just wanted to know how he did it. Watching Sir Thomas Browne with Diane reminds me it's okay to let go of the how and just enjoy the performance for what it is: pure entertainment.

"You think Grand Illusions sells this trick?" Diane jokes. "I could use a fishbowl with everlasting coins."

"Coins we can use to play the jukebox at the diner," I say. Diane agrees.

Soon enough, the fishbowl is filled to the brim and I'm in awe. What an amazing trick.

"And now, esteemed guests, our time together is quickly coming to an end," Sir Thomas Browne announces. "Before we depart, I think it's important we address the elephant in the room."

Diane and I look at each other. What is he talking about?

"You have been staring at my hat. It's hard not to. This hat has been with me for centuries," he says. "Remember, I'm quite the time traveler, and if I recall correctly, only the finest haberdasher bestowed this particular top hat upon me."

Sir Thomas Browne twirls the hat up into the sky and manages to land it right back on his head.

"For this next trick, I will need another assistant," he says. "Who wants to help this time traveler close out the show?

"Well, what about you—the lady with the short hair and black-and-white striped shirt." Sir Thomas Browne points in our direction. I didn't even notice when Diane raised her hand to volunteer.

"Way to go, Diane!" I cheer. I clap uncontrollably as she stands alongside Sir Thomas Browne. If only I had a camera to capture Diane making her debut as a magician's assistant. This is quite the auspicious occasion.

"I hope she's not allergic to animals," Derek says.

"Huh?" I say.

"Just you wait," he says mysteriously.

Sir Thomas Browne asks Diane to take a good look at his top hat.

"There's no rush. Give the topper a proper examination," he says. "I like to be thorough in these times, don't you? Tell me, Diane, what do you do?"

Diane examines the top hat for any holes or hidden pockets—anything out of the ordinary.

"I work at Wax Lips," she says, looking under the brim. "The record store."

After she checks the hat for a few more seconds, Sir Thomas Browne takes it back.

"Ah, then you must be a musical connoisseur. If you could play music right now, what song would you play?"

Diane presses her finger to her cheek and thinks hard. "Hmmm. I would play 'You've Got the Magic Touch' by the Platters, followed by 'It's Magic' by Doris Day."

The audience agrees and claps for Diane, as do I. Loudly!

"The perfect musical accompaniment for our times. As a young lad growing up in the verdant English countryside, I recall many a time listening to the tranquil sounds of the piano played by my mum."

As Sir Thomas Browne says this, he begins to move the hat from one hand to the other. He then collapses the hat down and brings it back to life again.

"Now tell me, Diane, why are you hiding that carrot?"

Diane smiles in a confused way. "I don't have a carrot."

Sir Thomas Browne looks just as confused as Diane. "Are you sure? This isn't yours."

He lightly taps behind Diane's right ear and produces a rather large carrot from thin air.

"Do you mind holding this for a second?" He hands the carrot to Diane. "Are you hungry? Good. We might need that."

Diane giggles. Sir Thomas Browne places the hat on a small table.

"And now I will just tap the hat once, twice, and…"

Sir Thomas Browne places his hand deep into the hat. When he pulls his hand out, he comes up… empty-handed.

"Umm, excuse me," Sir Thomas Browne says. "One second."

He does it once more. One tap. Two taps. Nothing! Something is wrong. Diane grimaces beside him. Derek stands. He knows something is wrong, too.

"I'm sorry. I'm missing something very important," Sir Thomas Browne says. His voice is cracking, changing.

"My beautiful bunny Esmeralda is missing! Where are ya, Esme?"

Suddenly, Sir Thomas Browne no longer has a British accent. In fact, he has a strong Brooklyn accent. He collapses to his knees and starts calling out for Esme.

"For gawd's sakes, where are you?"

Some audience members are laughing, thinking this is part of the show. I know it isn't. Not only is Sir Thomas Browne's bunny Esme missing but he's not even from the English countryside. What a time-traveling disaster!

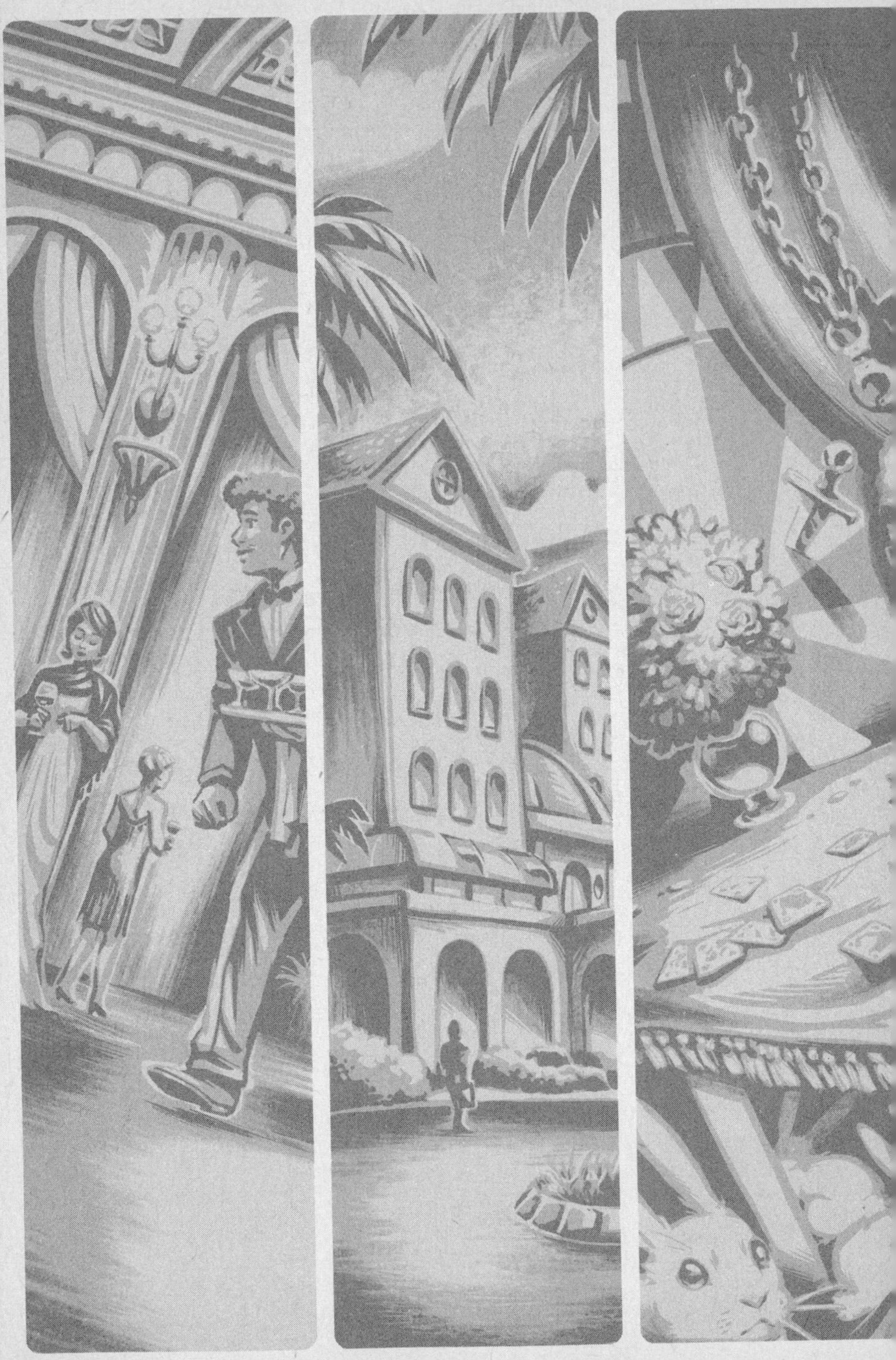

Chapter Eleven

"WHERE IS ESME? AND COCO? AND SNOWBALL?!"

Sir Thomas Browne shouts name after name. I'm guessing those bunnies were all meant to be in his act. The magician is a mess on the floor, searching for his beloved bunnies. There's not a shred of English nobility or the like from him, which makes the scene even more jarring.

"Who took her?"

Sir Thomas Browne has tears in his eyes, and that's my cue to get a handle on this situation. I run up to the stage and make a quick announcement.

"Folks, this show is at its end. Another magical performance can be found right across the way." I point to another show being conducted at the same time. "If you head over now, I'm sure you'll be able to catch the final act."

Diane is down on her knees, helping Sir Thomas Browne in his search.

"When's the last time you saw Esme?" Derek is behind me, already interviewing the distraught Sir Thomas Browne. I've got to put a stop to that. He's not the assistant house detective. I am!

"Derek, I think it's best you let me handle this," I say. "Why don't you go catch the next show?"

Derek places his hand on my shoulder.

"I don't think you understand. There won't be another show unless we find the culprit."

He may have a point. Still, it doesn't mean he's in charge of the Case of the Missing Props. It's never a good thing to allow a guest to be a part of the investigation. I mean, who's to say Derek Von Thurston is innocent? For all I know, he may be the culprit!

I kneel down to Sir Thomas Browne's level and offer a handkerchief for his tears. "I'm so sorry for this mix-up, Sir Thomas."

"You can call me Serge," he says. "The bunnies are my family, know-what-I-mean? True family."

Now that I'm this close to Sir Thomas Browne, I can see how the English accent obscured his full-on

New Yorker feel. Magicians are such interesting chameleons.

"What should we do?" Diane asks.

"There is something definitely happening at the Crossed Palms Resort," I say. "Mysteriousa was onto something. Sabotage may be at play."

"Mysteriousa?" Diane asks.

"Sorry, long story. I'll fill you in later. First, let me find Walt. Do you mind looking after Sir Thomas—I mean, Serge?"

I hop off the tiny stage and head into the hotel. No time for dillydallying. There are missing rabbits to rescue.

Hot on my heels is none other than Derek.

"Bunnies aren't an easy prop to steal," he says. "I think the first course of action should be to secure the perimeter and send out a search party."

"No, that's not what we're doing. You're a guest and should be relaxing," I say, trying to maintain an even tone. Derek's insistence on being my assistant is making it so hard for *me* to be *Walt's* assistant! "Did you know our resort has amazing pools? We do—we even have an Olympic-size one. A good soak in the pool would do wonders for a world traveler such as yourself."

Derek pulls out his pad. "Interesting reaction. I don't know many establishments that would ignore the catastrophe unfolding right before their eyes."

Oh no. Is he implying I'm not doing my job? I stop and turn to face him. He flashes a smug smile. His hand grips his pencil, ready to jot down whatever I'm about to say or do. Mom told me I should find compassion for Derek. He travels a lot and has to find ways to overcome his father's looming shadow. But this is too much.

"Now hold on one second, Derek. If there's one thing that's true about me above anything else, it's that I am solely dedicated to taking care of each and every person at the Crossed Palms Resort. That includes the bunnies, Serge, Professor Blaze, the movement magician, the Sorceress, and even you, Derek Von Thurston."

My voice may be carrying a bit in the hotel lobby because, before I can continue, Walt appears beside me.

"Is there a problem here?" he asks.

I want to scream, *Bugs Bunny and his family are missing, and Derek is questioning my job performance!*

But before I can give Walt the lowdown, Derek starts talking.

"You bet there is," he says, tapping his notepad. "The Case of the Missing Props has escalated to a full-on assault against magicians."

Walt looks like he's about to faint. Not only is Derek speaking way too loudly, thus drawing attention from onlookers scattered throughout the lobby, but he seems to be *enjoying* it.

"Walt, another incident has occurred," I say calmly. "Missing rabbits out in the garden."

Without any further explanation, Walt heads to the scene. Derek and I tag along behind him. In the garden, Diane and Sir Thomas Browne—Serge—are sitting at the edge of the stage. Serge dabs at his face with the handkerchief I gave him.

"How can I help?" Walt asks, and Serge recounts the whole trauma. Poor Serge. He loves those bunnies. Esme, Coco, and Snowball aren't just objets d'art. They are family.

"Where can they be?" he asks, trying hard to not break down again.

"We'll find them. We promise," Walt says. "If you don't mind, I'm going to ask you a few more questions."

I give Diane a nod and we take a few steps away from Walt and Serge. Derek doesn't take the hint, so I have to kind of nudge him away.

"Poor guy. What a horrible thing to happen," Diane says. "He's taken care of those bunnies since they were tiny. They live in a small house up in South Brooklyn. Bensonhurst, I believe."

"Did he tell you if he has any enemies?" Derek asks.

Diane cocks her head to the side. "Actually, he didn't because he was too busy being upset. Like we all are."

"Will you excuse us, Derek?" I say, pulling Diane away. Derek nods and continues to scribble in his notepad like a roving reporter.

"Wow. He's a little intense, isn't he?" Diane says.

"You can say that again," I say.

This has got to be the worst date ever. First, I had to cancel our romantic dinner. Then I took her to a magic show only to be a witness to foul play and Derek's incessant chattering. Everything about this date smells like a complete dud.

"I'm really sorry about everything. It looks like I have to work. I understand if you want to head out early."

Diane smiles a great big smile. "What are you talking about? I'm having the best time ever. Not only did I get to see wild magic being performed, but I'm right in the midst of a full-on mystery. I want to see this thing through just as much as you do."

My heart surges. Diane's right. Maybe this isn't so horrible. Our time together is full of action, intrigue, and even a little drama, courtesy of Derek.

"Thanks, Diane. I'll wait to see what Walt wants to do next. If only I had a clue as to where the bunnies went."

Diane looks to her left and right. "I didn't want to share this in front of Derek, but look at what Serge found."

Diane shows me a small hourglass.

"Serge swears he's never seen it before in his life. He doesn't use timers in his act."

Holy sand crystals. What does this mean? The person, or persons, committing these acts is leaving behind clues. This is someone who either wants to be caught or wants to outsmart the masses.

"It's as if the culprit is letting us know we're running out of time," I say.

"Or maybe that you're getting closer to the truth,"

Diane says. We both eyeball the timer and find nothing on it. No etches or initials. It doesn't even smell like anything—it's just a simple hourglass.

"The guilty party is speaking to us with these clues," I say. "I just need to find out how to decipher them."

"Goldie!"

Rob barrels over to us, screaming and waving his hands.

"Goldie! I've been looking all over for you," he says. He's out of breath and unable to formulate sentences.

"Breathe, Rob, or you're going to collapse right here and now," I say. I can't have missing bunnies *and* a fallen Rob.

"No time to breathe. Mr. Maple is heading over here, and he's on a rampage." Rob points back in the direction he's just come from. "It's him and Dr. Von Thurston. They're looking for you both."

"They're looking for me?" Diane asks. "I don't even know who they are."

Rob is holding on to his knees, trying to take in big breaths.

"No, Goldie and Walt," he says. "And hi, Diane. How's"—he gulps down some air—"it going?"

"No complaints, Rob," Diane says. "You should probably sit down."

"No time."

This is not good. Dr. Von Thurston and Mr. Maple are heading this way. Cheryl is in front of them, shaking her head vigorously in warning. Unfortunately, I have nowhere to run or hide.

"Well, Goldie, it looks like news travels fast," Derek says, now patting Rob on the back. "If you think I'm thorough, just wait until you hear from my dad. They don't call him the Renowned Showman for nothing."

"Dr. Von Thurston is walking over to us, and I don't know if I can make it," Rob says. Diane holds him upright. Serge lets out another moan over his lost bunnies, and Cheryl's eyes are about to bulge out of her head.

So much is happening I don't even know where to concentrate.

"Time's up," I say, and flip the sand timer.

The storm is about to hit.

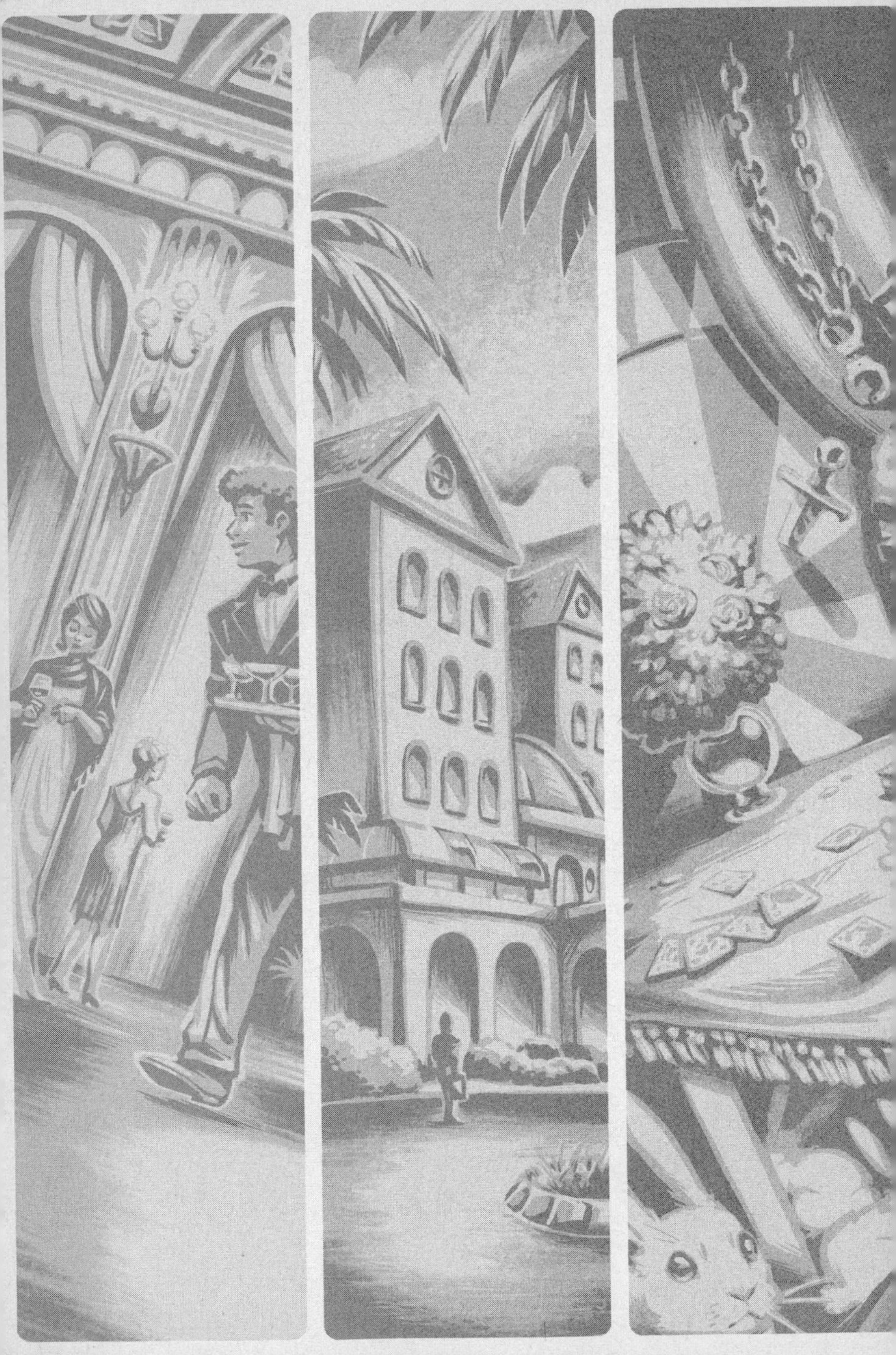

Chapter Twelve

"WALTER!" MR. MAPLE YELLS. POOR WALT PRACTICALLY jumps out of his skin from the noise. It's a good thing we're outside and most people are paying attention to the magic shows happening throughout the resort.

"Yes, Mr. Maple. I'm tending to one of our guests," he says, trying his best not to let his voice tremble.

Mr. Maple transforms his anger into the face we usually see him employ when he's in the public eye. The face of "everything is wonderful" and "smiles smiles smiles." On reflex, I start to grin, too. The one person who is not smiling is Serge, who continues to sniff back tears.

"I've been hearing things from Dr. Von Thurston here. Very disturbing things, in fact," Mr. Maple says. "And we need assurances that everything is on the up and up. Isn't it, Walt?"

"Well, umm, about that..." Walt stumbles and I can see he's in trouble.

"It sure is, Mr. Maple. Crossed Palms Resort is on the up, up, and uppiest," I say with as much enthusiasm as I can muster.

"Hello, Serge. How is New York treating you?" Dr. Von Thurston asks. "Apparently better than St. Pascal, from the looks of things."

Serge composes himself a tiny bit. "My bunnies. They're all gone."

Dr. Von Thurston places his hand on Serge's shoulder and gives it a small squeeze. Then he turns very rapidly, enough for his long cape to make a swishing sound. He is inches away from Mr. Maple.

"My son here has told me there are several props missing from various acts, including Ganapati's Chakra Cards and now Serge's bunnies," the magician says. Unlike Mr. Maple, Dr. Von Thurston doesn't raise his voice. Instead he speaks softly, elongating each word for emphasis. "This is unacceptable."

Rob starts to cough uncontrollably. I think his throat has gone dry from being so close to his idol. Diane goes to get him a glass of water before he completely collapses.

"It's true, Dr. Von Thurston. I've been speaking to witnesses," Derek announces. "I have many suspects but not enough evidence to point to the criminal mind behind it all."

"Tsk. Tsk. Tsk."

Dr. Von Thurston purses his lips with disapproval. This is not good. To have Derek, a VIP guest, alert Mr. Maple to all the things he's doing to help solve the case makes Walt and me look bad. Really bad.

"It is a sad state of affairs when my only son is having to give me a full report of the failings occurring in this establishment," Dr. Von Thurston says. "Do you not have people for this?"

Mr. Maple glares at Walt, who also starts coughing.

"Yes, sir. Some items have been misplaced, and Sir Thomas Browne—excuse me, Serge—has just notified us that part of his act has gone missing," Walt says.

"A big part of his act," Derek adds. "I would even say it's his whole act."

"I wouldn't say it's his whole act," Diane chimes in. Derek's remark is a bit of an insult to Serge. Why kick a man when he's already down? I don't like it and apparently Diane doesn't, either.

"Thank you," Serge says.

"Regardless, is it really true your bunnies have gone missing?" asks Dr. Von Thurston. Serge nods. "What is being done about this?"

Every time Dr. Von Thurston says something, Rob takes a small step toward him. It's barely noticeable, but Cheryl shakes her head each time he does it. Rob keeps rubbing his belly, presumably checking that his book is still safe and sound. I hope Rob has the mind to not ask for an autograph at this moment. Mr. Maple will have a full-on hissy fit if he does.

"Walt here is our house detective. He hasn't failed me once. I'm sure he has a plan, some important next steps we will be taking to locate the missing items and ensure all is well," Mr. Maple barks. "Right, Walt?"

"The plan is to conduct a thorough examination, interview those who set up the stage, and be proactive in making sure this doesn't happen to the other shows."

"I've already spoken to several workers," I say.

Mr. Maple gives me a scowl. I know exactly what's going on in his big brain. He's questioning why I'm interviewing anyone. Mr. Maple probably also wants to know why I'm not in the valet station parking cars. Then he notices Rob, who has taken yet another step toward Dr. Von Thurston. Rob freezes like a deer in headlights.

"It might be best to take this conversation inside, where I can order room service and we can talk this through calmly," Cheryl says. She truly understands the severity of the situation. Mr. Maple is about to yell at someone, and that someone is most likely going to be as follows: Rob, me, then Walt.

Walt tries to maneuver the group back inside, but Dr. Von Thurston isn't moving. Neither is Derek.

"I want to be perfectly clear. I will not, I repeat, will not take the stage if my act is jeopardized in some form or manner," Dr. Von Thurston says. "I have a reputation to uphold, and if this establishment is unable to meet the standards needed for me to do so, I simply won't risk it."

And with that, Dr. Von Thurston swooshes his cape and departs. His son soon follows. Sensing Mr. Maple is about to explode, Cheryl gently takes ahold of Serge and directs him to the entrance. Rob, looking a little lost now that Dr. Von Thurston has departed, also makes his exit. The only people left to witness this outburst will be me, Walt, and Diane. And I don't want Diane to bear witness to this mayhem.

"Diane, do you mind…"

Before I can finish the question, she gives me a wink and walks to the far end of the garden at a quick clip. I'm sorry to watch her go. I hope she doesn't fully leave the resort. This can't be how our date ends.

"*Walt!* This won't do at all!" Mr. Maple screams so loudly a few guests look our way with concern. He notices and lowers the volume a bit. If only he would employ the Dr. Von Thurston way of speaking. "Do you understand he's our featured performer? Do you understand the ramifications of him not getting onstage tomorrow? Talk about reputation! Securing this convention took years of schmoozing. This was a test run for the idea of the Crossed Palms Resort being the convention's yearly host. We can't afford for these mishaps to continue!"

Walt shakes with every word Mr. Maple says. As nervous as he looks, I know he's well into figuring out how to make this right. He's good at what he does, and that's why he's my mentor. Although Mr. Maple is yelling, this is just a lot of barking. The real work will happen as soon as Mr. Maple leaves.

"I am confident we will find the culprit before Dr. Von Thurston makes it to the stage."

"You better, or it will be your head," Mr. Maple says.

When Mr. Maple finally takes his leave, I can breathe. Did Mr. Maple happen to catch the workshop "How to Remove Your Head and Other Illusions"? Because he's taking things a little too on the nose—or head, I should say.

"Three bunnies," Walt says. He takes his glasses off and presses the bridge of his nose. Then he fixes his red hair and puts his glasses back on. "You heard the man. We've got to figure this out before tomorrow. What have we got so far?"

Walt and I find a bench surrounded by blooming star jasmine. The fragrance calms us both. I share what I've found so far, including the flash paper, the rabbit's foot, and now the hourglass. Walt scratches his head.

"Interesting. There might be a connection. What could it be?"

We watch the sand timer while we rack our brains.

"Maybe it's a road map. A hint of where they'll strike next," Walt says.

"That's what I was thinking, too," I say. "It's as if they *want* to be caught. Or maybe it's a way of showing off how they can outsmart the magicians."

"Are there any acts that have to do with time?"

"Serge is supposed to be a time traveler, but he's already been hit!"

"Hmmm." Walt ponders for a moment. "Let's think about this from another angle, then. What do we know about motives?" Walt asks. "Most people are motivated by money. Sometimes people can also be motivated by being validated. Seen."

Hmmm. A person could go to all this trouble just to be seen. If I feel ignored, I have a loud enough voice to make myself heard. In a world of magicians vying for attention, how do you stand out?

I pull out the schedule of the magic shows. In a few minutes, the first set will end and then there will be a break. During that break, the schedule lists a get-together for magicians, illusionists, big performers, and more to connect and unwind. Afterward, there's a headlining show featuring the Great Bradinski and his lovely assistant, Penelope.

Wait. His lovely assistant, Penelope. That gets me thinking.

"Evan mentioned something to me earlier. He said the assistants do all the work," I say. "Who wants to be seen or heard more than assistants? Maybe I should interview them."

Walt nods in agreement. "You're thinking some-one might be jealous of the acts? That's not a bad call."

I go back to the agenda. "There's an assistant get-together: the 'Now You See Us, Now You Don't Soiree.' I'll ask around. Get the feel of what's happening." It's the perfect time to do it. A jealous assistant or two might show up to the party to brag.

"We can't just assume that this is the work of a jealous assistant. This could also be the work of a magician out to make a name for themselves. Per-haps a smaller player in the field," Walt explains. "I'll have Cheryl give me a list of magicians, and I'll begin asking around. If there's a hierarchy at play here among the magicians, we should know about it immediately."

We both stand up, ready to get on with it.

"Under no circumstances are you to allow Derek to assist you in this investigation," Walt says.

Derek! If there's anyone who is trying to stand out, it's him.

"Not only is he a straight source to his father, but he may have his own agenda," Walt explains.

"I didn't ask Derek to help me," I say, slightly annoyed. "He just sort of forced his way."

"Funny." Walt chuckles. "Isn't that what you do all the time?"

I want to argue and tell him that I'm not even one iota like Derek, but Walt has already walked away to start his part of the investigation.

No, sir. I am not like Derek at all. And I'm not about to let him sabotage my love of solving mysteries.

I try to compose myself. Why get worked up over nothing? Derek is nowhere to be found at the moment. I need to take advantage of that and get a head start on the interviews.

But first, I've got to find Diane.

Chapter Thirteen

I HEAD IN THE DIRECTION DIANE WENT BEFORE MR. Maple began his screaming rampage. The workshops are over by now, and the garden is filled with roving magicians, fans, and the like. Soon, they will disperse into various get-togethers and meetups throughout the resort. Each party will be equipped with a bar and appetizers to tide people over before the bigger entertainment tonight.

I cross the garden and take a turn toward a tiny bridge where guests can look at a trickling waterfall. It's a perfect place to enjoy the beautiful weather. And it's exactly where I find Diane, leaning against the railing of the bridge and calmly staring at the waterfall. Rays of soft golden sunlight are highlighting her face. I stop and stare for a second. I hope she's having at least a bit of a good time. I can't help feeling responsible for ruining her afternoon.

"Hey, Diane."

"Hey, Goldie!" she says. "How are you holding up? Your boss seemed to have a few choice words to share."

I brush it off. "Mr. Maple? I'm used to it," I say. "Some men like to walk around in a storm because they think they get more done that way. It usually doesn't work."

"There's no excuse for it," Diane says. "I take it you're officially back on the clock?"

I nod. "It sure seems that way. I've got to head out soon to speak to some magicians' assistants. We should probably reschedule," I say, trying my hardest not to sound as glum as I feel. I would much rather hang out with Diane than work, but when I think of those poor bunnies and Serge's distraught expression, the urge to solve this mystery intensifies. I can only hope Diane understands.

"I don't mind tagging along—that is, if you want me to."

Do I? I want to scream. I play it cool instead, as cool as this goofy grin plastered across my face can allow.

"Great! There will be small bites, so you won't go

hungry," I say. "And if you get bored, you can leave. I won't be offended one bit."

Diane places her hand over mine.

"Cool."

For a moment the world sort of stands still. I imagine my magnifying glass, Mr. Oculus, jumping out of my pocket and very carefully studying her hand. Is this really happening?

Then I think of the bunnies with their cute bunny faces being scared and snap back to the task at hand.

"Cool. Cool. Cool."

Oh God, I can't stop saying *cool*. Get it together, Marigold Vance.

"'The Now You See Us, Now You Don't Soiree.' That's what the party is called," I say. "I can only hope the bunnies will show up, too, hippity hopping along."

I lead Diane across the bridge and make a quick cut to the back of the hotel. The soiree is being held in one of the conference rooms. As we walk past other party rooms, we notice how each of them has been decorated with a certain theme. There's a room with people flinging their capes around dramatically. It's as if they're dueling to find who has the flashiest cape swoosh. In another room, several magicians are slow dancing to the Drifters singing "This Magic Moment." We pause at the entrance and sway to the glorious music for just a few seconds.

We find the room we're looking for—the location of the "Now You See Us, Now You Don't Soiree." The room is filled with beautiful young women in sequin gowns. A couple of men punctuate the scene, but for the most part it's a ladies' soiree. I walk in and see Cheryl and Rob watching two magicians in a corner of the room. We join them.

"What's going on?" I whisper to Cheryl.

"They call it jamming."

I am thoroughly confused. I thought jamming was when musicians got together to play music, freestyling off each other to see what they can come up with. This is different.

Two young assistants are performing together. First, one does a trick; then the other plays off that trick and performs another, in a kind of riff on the previous trick.

"Dueling magicians!" I say.

Rob corrects me. "Not necessarily. Just two magicians exchanging ideas."

Even better. We watch as the two magicians

continue to perform various tricks. They're both women, which adds to the brilliance of it all. Each time one of them finishes a trick, we clap. They're doing this for fun, and their enjoyment is contagious. I get so caught up in their jamming I forget what I'm supposed to be doing.

For the love of Esme, Coco, and Snowball, I must focus and start my job! I leave Diane with the others and begin my process. First, I give the soiree a good once-over. Several jam sessions are occurring at the same time. A few intimate conversations are taking place. Some people are pouring themselves drinks.

"On your right, Goldie." Arnold, a server, pauses by me with a trayful of mini cucumber sandwiches. "I thought you had the day off?"

I grab one of the cucumber sandwiches and pop it into my mouth. "A detective's work is never done," I say. "Arnold, have you noticed anything unusual happening? Any bunnies hopping about?"

"Bunnies? The only thing I've seen are magic tricks everywhere. No bunnies. Sorry, Goldie."

I take one more cucumber sandwich and eat it before heading toward two women clinking their glasses together in a toast. One of the ladies wears a glamorous, snug dress in electric blue, while the other wears a flashy and short red dress with a top hat. I can't help being drawn to the top hat. It looks similar to the one Serge wore. But who am I kidding? If I take a quick look around, there's a whole lot of top hats happening. It's the fashion du jour.

"And I said, that's the queen of hearts!" the woman in electric blue says while the other laughs.

"Good evening! My name is Goldie, and I'm the assistant house detective here at the Crossed Palms Resort." Before I can continue, the woman with the top hat interrupts.

"You're an assistant, too! Welcome to the club," she says, raising her glass for another toast. "May we shine as brightly as the men who tend to hog the spotlight."

"Oh, Betty, don't be so hard."

"You're right. At least my boss isn't as bad as—"

"Betty! You don't want to give this young one the wrong idea about being an assistant," the other woman says before taking a big sip from her glass.

"Rose, you and I both know the unsung heroes are the assistants," Betty says. She turns to me. "Wouldn't you agree?"

I nod. I guess this may be the case to a certain

degree, and maybe that's a good enough reason for someone to wreck a trick or two. Walt always makes sure everyone is aware of my contributions. He doesn't hog the limelight. In fact, he dreads it.

"It sure can be hard, working with such bigger-than-life personalities," I say. "Hard enough to want to mess up an act, I bet! I mean, I wouldn't do that. Would you?"

The two give each other a sly glance.

"Just between us gals, we're talking about the missing props, aren't we?" Rose says. I totally appreciate how she is whispering. "We've heard all about it, and of course fingers are being pointed toward us, but you're barking up the wrong tree."

Betty cocks her eyebrow high and whispers: "There's always the rumor of someone conveniently forgetting a prop or two. Or fumbling what they were meant to be doing," she says. "Remember Trudie in Chicago? That was a doozy of a failure."

Rose whistles. "Do I? All the assistants got flak for it. As if we would ever."

"Never!" Betty says emphatically. "You've got to understand, Goldie. Assistants have an unspoken rule we abide by: We do our job no matter what because our love for magic and entertaining is true."

I pause. "What about if someone is just plain angry or jealous?"

"Ask all the assistants here, and they'll tell you the same thing," Rose says. "The love for magic supersedes everything, even when working with overly demanding personalities. If you don't love magic, then you are not a true magician."

Food for thought.

"Also, none of those magicians who lost props have assistants," Betty adds. "They only do solo work."

I hadn't thought about that. Ganapati appeared on the stage by himself. Professor Blaze was with Mysteriousa, but she's not his assistant. And Serge was alone, minus his missing bunnies.

"You're right," I say.

"Of course we are! We assistants know everything," Betty says, tapping her top hat. "Ask around and you'll hear the same story. We haven't heard a thing about an assistant causing this much damage. If we did, we would have been all over it."

"Like breaking news," Rose adds. "We are a very tight-knit community. Nothing gets past us. Right, Betty?"

"Thanks for your valuable insight, ladies," I say. "I

have a hot tip for you both: Eat the cucumber sandwiches. They're refreshing."

I walk to another group of assistants, and they relay the same message. There have been no rumors of unhappy assistants undermining acts, not recently anyway. It doesn't matter how many people I speak to; they all say the same thing. The props weren't stolen by an assistant staying at the Crossed Palms Resort.

"Magicians love dramatic flair," says a male assistant. "Who doesn't? Hijacking bunnies is a line we just would never cross. There's a Magician's Code of Ethics that states, and I quote, 'Promote the humane treatment and care of livestock used in magical performance.'" The assistants bow their heads in silence.

"But surely an assistant would be willing to make their boss look bad...."

I recognize the voice right away. It's not Rob or Cheryl or Diane, all three of whom are having a good time with Rose and Betty in a corner of the room. It's not Walt or even Mr. Maple, who would surely be yelling about something. No, the voice belongs to the one and only Derek Von Thurston. Talk about crossing a line.

"Oh, look who's arrived," Betty says. "C'mon, Rose,

I think we need another drink." The other assistants follow Betty to the bar. I'm sure I'm not the only one noticing the frosty reception Derek is receiving. I bet it has more to do with his father than with him. Either way, he seems unfazed. He insists on speaking to other assistants, but their responses are curt.

"You're not supposed to be interviewing Crossed Palms guests," I say. I try to rein in my anger. "That's *my* job."

Derek sniffs. "It's hard to tell whether or not you're working the Case of the Missing Props. As a part-time detective, it's imperative I lend a hand before my father's big show."

Cheryl notices our heated conversation and walks over. Rob and Diane follow.

"It's up to the hotel staff to contain the situation," Cheryl says in a very professional hotel voice. "We ask you to allow Goldie and Walter Tooey to perform their jobs. We are here to quell any worries you may have."

"Well, ummm, Cheryl," Derek says. "My father will not perform unless the culprit or culprits are detained. Walt and Goldie clearly can't do this alone. As a representative of the acclaimed Dr. Von Thurston, I respectfully believe you need my help."

"He does have a point," Rob says. The stone face both Cheryl and I give him causes him to shrink slightly. "There is no *I* in *team*."

Et tu, Rob?

"He *is* a part-time detective," Rob reiterates, albeit in a timid voice. He must notice the flames shooting from the tops of our heads.

"I'm assuming you'll be attending the Great Bradinski's show," Derek says. "So am I! We can sit together."

"I just…I can't. Ugh!" I grab Diane's and Cheryl's hands and head toward the exit.

As expected, Derek and Rob immediately follow. We manage to pick up the pace and leave the guys behind us.

"I can't believe Rob," Cheryl says.

"I can't believe Derek," I say.

"I can't believe I'm going to see a magician who goes by the name of the Great Bradinski," Diane says. "How many *great* Bradinskis have you met in your lifetime? Honestly, none that I can think of."

And with that, the urge to laugh takes over my body. I can't help it. Diane is so excited to see more magic. Soon my anger slowly melts away. The Great

Bradinski. She's right—I've never met a *great* Bradinski before. Who knows what we can expect from his show?

Who cares if Derek and Rob are driving me bananas? I've got Cheryl and Diane beside me. Soon we'll be watching the Great Bradinski in action, and I can only hope we will get even closer to solving this mystery.

Since Cheryl and I know everyone, we're able to cut past the long line to enter the show. We score front-row seats, enough for us all to sit, even Derek.

"Keep your eyes and ears open. Something is about to happen," I say. "I can feel it in my bones."

My thoughts are churning with everything the assistants shared with me. I might not be closer to solving this brain twister, but I am definitely eliminating motives.

"Mr. Bradinski," I say, "I await your greatness."

Chapter Fourteen

ROB AND DEREK TAKE THE SEATS BESIDE US.

"Do you think your father will join us?" Rob asks. "Should we save him a seat?"

Derek shakes his head. "I'm his eyes and ears," he says. "Besides, I know all there is to know about the Great Bradinski. I've seen every single magician perform countless times. Since I was a little kid, magicians have been part of my life."

"That sounds like the perfect life for me," Rob says.

"Sure is," Derek says.

Do I note a hint of weariness in his tone? I'm reminded once again of what Mom said to me. *It must be hard to live in his father's shadow all the time.* It also gets me thinking about how wreaking havoc on certain magic shows could garner Derek his father's attention. Hmmm. The one person I need to interrogate is the one person I've been trying to avoid. Now, this is no simple task. I'll have to play off what Derek loves.

He comes from this magical world. Years of being around so many illusionists, conjurors, and enchanters have made him an expert, even if his *expertise* can be overbearing. I have to stop viewing him as an annoying pest and start utilizing his knowledge.

"How big of a deal is the Great Bradinski?"

Derek can't shake the surprised look from his face. I guess he didn't expect me to actually ask him a question. He's probably used to just spouting out facts at all hours of the day to anyone in direct contact with him. But maybe it's the exact opposite. What if living with a father as big and famous as Dr. Von Thurston causes a person to shrink their personality? What if the only time Derek gets to shine is when he's with strangers, people who don't know a thing about his father (minus Rob, of course)?

Who knows?

"He's obviously not as big as my father, but he draws in the crowds, as you can tell," he says. "The Great Bradinski is a graduate of the traditional school of escapology. He has followed the footsteps of the great Davenport brothers, Australia's very own illusionist Murray, and of course the renowned Harry Houdini."

"Of course, Houdini!" Rob says. "He's the guy who practically created magicians."

Derek tsk-tsks Rob's statement. He's mimicking his father's reaction from earlier in the day. "Harry Houdini was *not* the first magician. He happened to be at the right time and place. Some people are just lucky."

He sounds disgruntled. Derek can't hide his disdain for anyone who isn't his father.

"Derek, remind me where you were this morning at around eight AM?" I ask as casually as possible.

While not quite diabolical, the laugh Derek delivers almost reaches that level. I have to hand it to him. He must practice his cackle in the mirror to get it just right. It starts off quiet and then at the end he really brings up the noise. It's long lasting and goes way beyond proving a point. Both Diane and Cheryl place their hands over their ears. I don't. I take in every single high and low octave until he eventually stops.

"We've already established this. I was having

breakfast with Dr. Von Thurston," he says after what seems like a lifetime of laughter. "Everyone at the restaurant can verify that."

Diane shrugs beside me. It would be easy to confirm Derek's morning appointment. Still.

"What was the name of your server?" I ask. "Anyone who can actually verify you were there?"

"You can ask any of the assistants," he quickly responds. "A bunch of them were eating at a table together across the way. I remember because when I said good morning to them, they simply nodded."

"What is it between you and the assistants?" I ask.

"You'll have to ask them that question."

"Maybe I will!"

"Did Dr. Von Thurston enjoy his breakfast? Did he order eggs, too?" Rob asks.

Cheryl sharply elbows him.

"Never mind," Rob says. "It's a weird question to ask."

I'll make sure to verify Derek's morning alibi later. I need to bring this running train back on track. I pull the hourglass out of my pocket.

"What do escape artists need compared to other magicians?" I ask.

"The element of time, of course," Derek says. He

reaches for the hourglass. "The crown jewel of the Great Bradinski's act revolves around escaping from a straitjacket before the wooden case he stands on goes up in flames. And he gives himself only five minutes."

"Hmmm."

"The guilty party left this behind, didn't they?" he asks. "Did you dust for fingerprints?"

"Too many people handled the piece to be able to pull out a good set of prints," I say. Serge found the hourglass, Diane touched it, and then she handed it to me. Dusting for prints wouldn't have made a difference.

"Too bad," he says.

"Why would the culprit leave this behind?" I say. "You say escapologists must escape from their trick in a timely fashion."

"Yes," he says.

"Hmmm."

Everyone stares at the timer. The Great Bradinski is the only magician performing tonight, and if his big trick involves escaping from a straitjacket, then whoever is sabotaging the act will surely be...

"I've got to use the restroom," I say. "I'll be right back."

I get up, taking the hourglass with me. I walk to the

back of the ballroom toward the exit. Before leaving, I quickly glance around. Derek is straining his neck to make sure I'm heading to the bathroom. It's smart of him not to trust me. He'll be disappointed to see I really *am* entering the ladies' restroom. But he doesn't know the Crossed Palms Resort the way I do. Let him believe I'm going to the restroom. I have to check something of the utmost importance.

When I enter the restroom, I greet Erika, the bathroom attendant. Erika takes her duties seriously. She is quick to offer a guest a mint or a tiny spritz of flowery perfume. If you're in need of a little touch-up of makeup, Erika loves to suggest the right color of blush or lipstick. This restroom is right next to the ballroom. It's extremely busy, and Erika makes sure no one is ever lacking a beauty essential.

"Hi, Erika. Busy night, huh?"

Erika does not respond. The key to being a bathroom attendant is anticipating your guest's needs and doing so as quietly as possible.

"Do you mind opening the side door for me? I forgot something and want to avoid the crowd outside."

Erika communicates by eyeing the bathroom sink. Although I didn't use the restroom, she wants to see me wash my hands. Erika is a stickler for cleanliness. She hums to the tune of Buddy Holly's "Everyday" while I wash my hands thoroughly until the song ends. When I'm done, she hands me a towel to dry and turns to open the side entrance. This particular bathroom has a door that leads to the back of the ballroom via one of the hotel's many intricate hallways.

"Thanks, Erika!" I say. In the hallway, I take a sharp right toward the back of the ballroom, where the Great Bradinski should be preparing to step onto the stage any minute now. I walk fast and with serious purpose. I need to do all this before Derek starts to wonder what's taking me so long.

A couple of security guards are situated by the backstage door. They're people I know. It's good to see Walt is being proactive about the saboteurs striking again. Since I know them, the guards just open the door and let me waltz in.

Backstage is a whole other world. Various hotel workers are creating their own behind-the-scenes magic. Setting. Lights. People ready to pull up the heavy velvet curtains. No one bats an eye when I walk past them. They're used to me lurking about. I make sure not to trip over any of the heavy ropes or wires.

I quickly reach my destination. We like to call the room I'm currently facing the pink room because the walls are a bright shade of pink. Mr. Maple wanted to call the backstage dressing rooms something other than green rooms to stand out among other hotels. It's fine by me. Pink or green, it doesn't matter. The Great Bradinski is behind this door.

Unfortunately, the men guarding the pink room refuse to open it for me.

"Sorry, Goldie. Strict orders from the Great Bradinski. No one is allowed in, under any circumstances," one says. "He said something about secrets being revealed."

"What if it's an emergency?" I ask. Which it is. I want to make sure everything is on the up and up. Knowing what I know now about how important time is to the Great Bradinski's trick, I think the hourglass means someone could have already sabotaged his act.

"I need to warn the magician," I say. "This is a big deal."

The guard doesn't budge. I appreciate his commitment to the job. Loyalty to doing the right thing is an admirable quality...except when it gets in my way. I have to persuade him to let me in.

A light bulb goes off in my head.

"I got it! What if I'm blindfolded? I won't be able to see what the Great Bradinski is doing," I say. That's not ideal, but drastic times mean drastic measures. The Great Bradinski wants to make sure no one discovers how his tricks are performed. If I can't see what's happening, then his tricks stay safe with him, and I can talk to him without compromising his work.

"All I need is for one of you guys to tie my headband over my eyes, open the door, and push me gently into the room," I say. "It's all I'm asking."

The guard scratches the back of his head. "I don't know, Goldie."

I take my headband out of my hair and place it over my eyes.

"Just tie it like so. Then knock on the door," I say. "Easy breezy."

Eventually, the guard relents. He secures the headband to my face and gives the door a series of knocks. My guess is that it's a secret code of some sort. Without my eyesight, I have to rely on my other senses. Lucky for me, I know the pink room well enough. Hopefully I won't bump into anything.

"You may enter!" a woman's voice says. The door opens, and I take two very short steps forward.

"Who are you?" the woman says. "Oh, didn't I speak to you earlier, during the assistants' soiree?"

Her voice sounds familiar, but I can't immediately place it. It's definitely not Rose or Betty. Those two had very distinct accents.

"Yes! I did attend that party. My name is Goldie, and I'm the Crossed Palms Resort's assistant house detective."

A puff of perfume suddenly fills the air. She must have just spritzed herself. I also hear the sound of someone moving things around—a chair scraping against the floor. A squeaky sound of a shoe.

"We've already spoken to the house detective. A man named Walter Tooey."

The Great Bradinski speaks, I bet.

"He's my boss. I'm here to ask you a couple of questions."

There's another scrape of a chair. Another squeaky sound. The other shoe being put on, perhaps?

"We're on in less than five minutes, and I have a blindfolded girl in a bright-pink room," he says. "If I weren't the Great Bradinski, I would think this was some sort of practical joke."

"No joke, sir. Just trying to do my job," I say. "See,

I've been thinking. The timing is going to be way off when it comes to your act."

"What do you know about my act? I've never performed in St. Pascal before today. I've performed this act hundreds, maybe even *thousands*, of times. I can even do it blindfolded. No one will mess up my act. Impossible."

"Sorry, Great Bradinski. If my gut is right, I think someone has already rigged your act to fail, and I can prove it."

The room goes eerily quiet. No squeaky sounds of shoes being put on. No scraping of a chair on the floor. One thing is for sure: The seconds are slowly ticking away, and I'm standing before the Great Bradinski solely on a hunch. I hope I'm wrong.

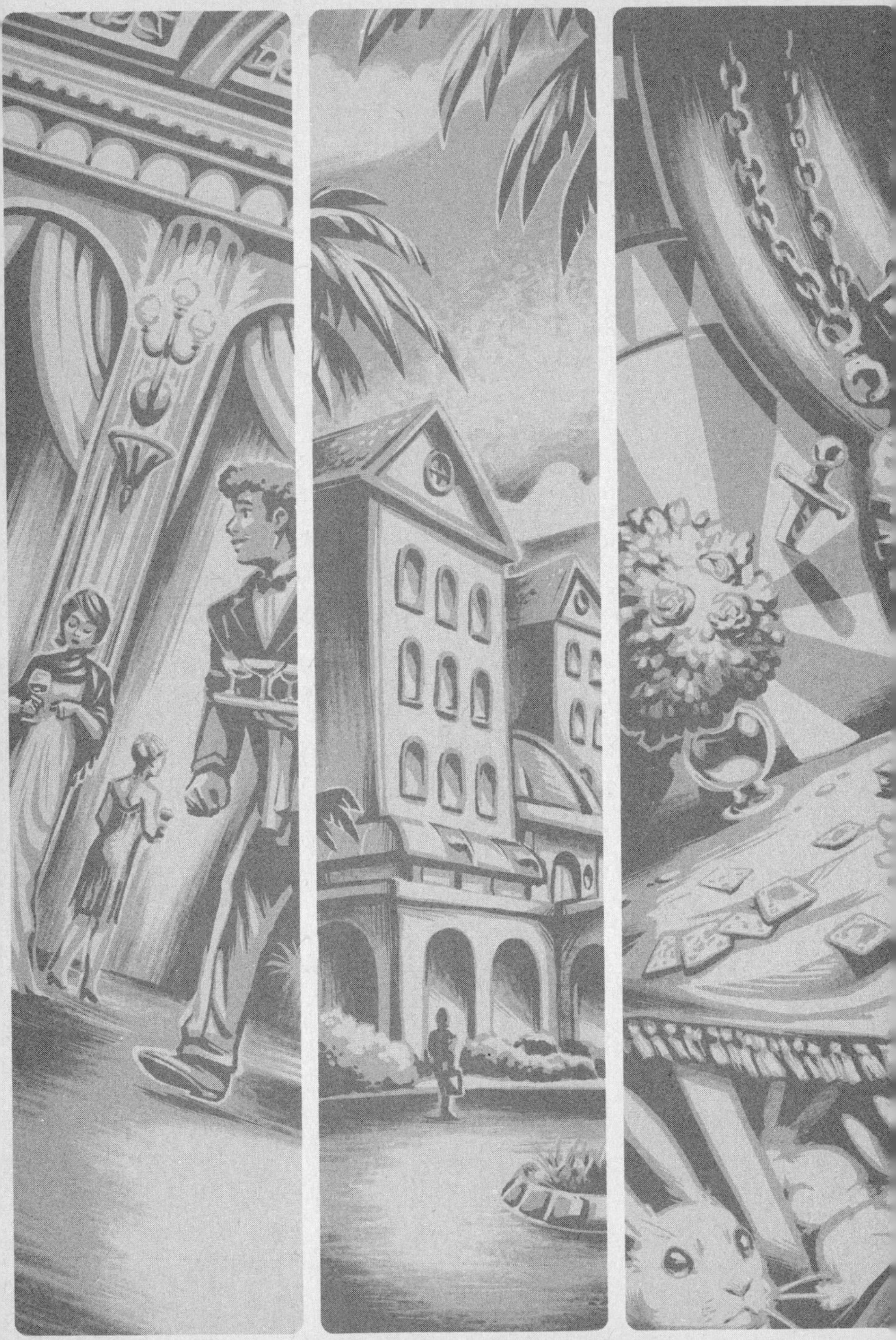

Chapter Fifteen

"FIVE MINUTES TO CURTAIN," A VOICE SAYS.

I don't have much time. I need to take off this blindfold and show the Great Bradinski what I'm talking about. I don't know if I'm right, but I feel like I am.

"Sir, if you will just indulge me for a second. My expertise is in mysteries. I believe your straitjacket has been compromised." I take another small step. "If you'll let me show you and we find nothing wrong, then no harm done. But if I'm right…"

A loud sigh in front of me. Someone's heels walking behind me. And a couple of seconds later, my blindfold is loosened. It takes a moment for my eyes to adjust, but there he is. The Great Bradinski stares at me, his bushy eyebrows gathered together in concern.

"I am the Great Bradinski, and this is my assistant,

Penelope." I give a short wave to Penelope as she crosses the room. "You mentioned my straitjacket. It's been my tool for many years."

"As have these." Penelope opens a wardrobe case full of identical straitjackets—each exactly the same as the next, or so it seems. They must have a rig that allows the Great Bradinski to escape. I bet every single one of them is faulty.

"Now, why should I divulge my trick to a girl, let alone a stranger?"

"I'm not just any girl. I'm the assistant house detective, and my job is to make sure sabotage has not contaminated this room," I say. "You've heard what's happened to the other acts. I don't want the same to happen to yours."

He examines my face. Really studies it. I stand tall, with my hands pressed against my sides. My chin slightly raised. There's a long pause, and I'm nervous we're running out of time.

"Swear to me right here and right now you will not divulge my secret," the Great Bradinski says. "In the name of the great magician John Nevil Maskelyne, who founded the Occult Committee that I am a member of, you must swear."

I place my hand over my heart. "I don't know who John Nevil Maskelyne is, nor do I know what the Occult Committee does, but I do swear by all the famous detectives, including Miss Marple, Walt Tooey, and Sherlock Holmes."

A detective is no good if they can't be trusted to keep their word. I don't make promises I can't keep.

Convinced by my swearing, the Great Bradinski shows me the straitjacket. The jacket has so many straps and buckles. I wouldn't even know how to put it on. It is one complicated piece of clothing.

"Every straitjacket act is different. Some people love to tell stories and misdirect the audience with tales," he says. "Others love using flash paper and dramatic music. I am a purist. No elaborate gimmicks. Just a man with a ticking clock, completely strapped into a jacket."

He holds the jacket by the hanger and twirls it around so we can get a real good look at it.

"Regardless of how you go about performing the act, there is always one thing most magicians agree upon," he says. "The trick, if you will, is this: To convince the audience that I cannot simply unfasten these straps by manipulating my body, Penelope places a lock. An added dramatic flair."

He shows me a lock. It seems normal, not too big or cumbersome, with a slot underneath for a tiny key to unlock it. Right now the lock hangs off one of the sleeves of the jacket.

"I always have a key placed in a secret compartment," the Great Bradinski says. "A different compartment in each of the straitjackets. The key is how I'm able to escape. For this particular jacket, it's in here."

The magician inserts his finger into the tiniest of slots in the back of the jacket.

"It is always here...."

He digs some more. Twirls the jacket again. Lo and behold, the key is missing!

The Great Bradinski grabs another jacket and searches it. No key! Then another. And another.

Blinding pink room, I was right!

"Unbelievable!" he says. "All the keys are gone!"

A sudden pounding on the door startles us. An argument is occurring right outside the room.

"I'm Derek Von Thurston, and I demand to be let in!"

There is a bit of a crash and a thump. The door swings wide open and Derek comes tumbling in, landing flat on his face. Not the grand entrance I'm sure he's used to, but an entrance nonetheless.

"Bradinski, you're in trouble!" Derek says, barely able to speak coherently from the tussle.

"Well, son, you are a little too late with the news," the Great Bradinski says. He's holding up the last straitjacket, about to check it. We both know there will be no key. When the ugly truth is undeniable, the Great Bradinski slumps into a chair.

"Do you mind if I take a look around?" I ask. I climb over Derek, who is still on the floor, and walk to the wardrobe case. I look inside the portable closet, tap on the walls, and lift the small rug. I check under the Great Bradinski's shoes, which are lined up like soldiers at the bottom of his luggage. "Is this case always kept locked?"

"Of course. I unlocked it as soon as we got here," Penelope says. "We had to get ready."

"Then *you* must be the culprit!" Derek shouts at her. "How long have you been working for the Great Bradinski?" He stands and brushes himself off. Honestly, I wish he would just lie on the floor and keep quiet.

"Aren't you Dr. Von Thurston's son?" Penelope asks. "Why are you here?"

"I'm a concerned magician and part-time detective."

I stop him before his hand reaches into his pocket to pull out his card.

"Don't," I say, taking out my pad and pen. "Never mind him. How many people came to the room while you were here and the wardrobe was unlocked?"

"Plenty of people. Walt Tooey. The guards. A waiter. The director of the show. Lights people."

"A waiter?" I ask.

"The Great Bradinski insists on drinking hot chamomile tea before each performance," she says. "It helps calm his nerves."

She points to a rolling serving cart with a steaming pot of tea, sugar cubes, and mugs. I walk over to the cart and notice the mug with the recently poured tea. I keep searching, sensing the road is slowly narrowing. I always get a slight itch on the back of my neck when I'm getting closer to solving a mystery, and my neck is tingling like crazy.

I look underneath the rolling cart. A shiny object gleams brightly. I stretch my hand under the cart to try to dislodge the object, but Derek's thin fingers grab it before I can.

"*A coin!*" Derek exclaims.

"Give me that!" I say. "I found it first!"

I reach for the coin, but Derek has some sort of supernatural grip. He will not let go. Because I have completely lost all sense of time and place, I don't realize how Derek and I are now wrestling on the floor for the coin, right in front of the Great Bradinski and Penelope.

"Goodness," Penelope says. The Great Bradinski clears his throat loudly enough to bring me back to my senses. I sit up, having been able to secure the coin from Derek's sticky fingers.

"I'm so sorry," I say while I try to fix my yellow headband. Derek is testing all my patience. Lucky for him, I don't have time to show him my true brute strength.

"Is this your coin?" I ask.

Penelope shakes her head. "We've never seen this coin before," the Great Bradinski says. "Ever."

The last time I saw coins was during Serge's fishbowl trick, just a couple of hours ago. So many coins appearing out of thin air and falling into the bowl. I take a closer look. Those coins were different. Smaller.

I've seen this coin before, being tossed up in the air and landing in the palm of his hand. My heart races.

"Did the waiter have shaggy blond hair?" I ask.

The Great Bradinski and Penelope both nod.

"He was a little peculiar. He kept mumbling to himself about magic tricks," Penelope says. "I didn't pay him any mind."

"Because we went to our meditation space," the Great Bradinski says.

In a corner of the room is a small altar.

"We practice abraca-yoga," the magician says. "Before each show, for at least fifteen minutes. It helps limber the body. We felt it was important to practice after hearing what happened to our dear friend Ganapati."

"That's right. So we ended up extending our abraca-yoga practice to a half hour," Penelope adds. "We left the waiter as he set up the cart while we spent time over here."

More than enough time for Evan to quickly go through the wardrobe and take each of the keys. I hope I'm wrong, but Evan would have had access to all the performers whose props went missing. Their performance spaces had pitchers of water, iced tea, and whatever else the magicians asked to be served.

"I'm sorry this has happened. Would you like me to make an announcement to the audience about the show being canceled?"

The Great Bradinski stands up with a determined expression on his face.

"The Great Bradinski never cancels a show," he says. "Penelope, let them know we will be five minutes late."

Penelope goes to the door and speaks to the guards.

"How will you escape from the jacket?" Derek asks. "It won't be much of a show now, will it?"

The Great Bradinski walks over to Derek and places his hand on his shoulder. He does the same to me. Then he slowly leads us both to the door.

"The person who tried to sabotage my finale will not get the satisfaction of a job well done," he says. "I've been in this game far too long to let this slight bump stop me. No. The show must always go on. And to do so, I will need you both to leave."

"But…"

The Great Bradinski doesn't wait for Derek to say another word. He just allows the door to open for Penelope to walk through, and then he closes it in our faces.

And that marks the end of my time with the Great Bradinski and his fabulous assistant, Penelope. I wish he could have kept Derek with him. Oh well.

I've got to find Evan.

Chapter Sixteen

THE SHOW WILL GO ON, WHICH IS GOOD BECAUSE IT will buy me some time. I walk as quickly as possible, ignoring Derek's pleas for me to hear him out.

"Goldie, will you wait?!"

If Walt or my dad ever hears how I was wrestling with a hotel guest, they'll blow a gasket. I can't believe I allowed my emotions to get the best of me. But I had to secure the coin, didn't I?

"The coin!" Derek yells. "I've seen that coin before."

I stop in my tracks.

"What do you mean you've seen this coin before?" I say. "Where?"

"If you would just listen to me for one second, I can tell you." He takes a deep breath, but I simply cannot listen to another of his long-winded stories. I place my hand over his mouth.

"Keep the story short. We have to get somewhere."

Derek nods silently and I remove my hand from his face.

"Can I please see the coin?" he asks.

I hand him the gold piece.

"I knew it. This coin is from Sweden. It's a rare coin, distributed only a couple of years ago. A small box of these was given to Dr. Von Thurston as a gift when he traveled to perform for Swedish dignitaries," Derek says. "There were five coins in the leather box. One of them went missing."

"Missing?"

"He won't admit this publicly, but he has always employed assistants. He likes to call them 'mentees.' They're magicians he wants to help with their careers," Derek says. "However, he never shares the limelight with any of them. They're tasked to do what he says, when he says it, and in return he teaches them tricks."

Absentmindedly, Derek starts to manipulate the coin so that it travels across his knuckles. It's mesmerizing. I can't stop staring at the coin, moving effortlessly as if it has a mind of its own.

Derek lets out a long, pensive sigh.

"Sometimes Dr. Von Thurston treats these mentees like they're his children," he says quietly.

For the first time ever, I notice how painful it must be for him to have to compete for his father's attention.

The coin still slowly goes over his knuckles.

"One of his last mentees was a young guy with a military-style buzz cut, very short," Derek says.

Sigh. Evan doesn't have short hair at all. His hair is wild and shaggy. It practically covers his eyes.

"What was his name?" I ask.

"Evan."

My heart plunges. Shaggy hair be gone! It was Evan!

"Whatever happened to him?"

"What happens to every assistant he ever employs. He grows weary of their presence and starts to accuse them of wanting to take his place," he says. "Evan traveled with us to Sweden, where Dr. Von Thurston was going to be celebrated. Evan insisted Dr. Von Thurston allow him to perform alongside him. He felt he had learned all there was to learn about magic and should be allowed to prove it at the coin-giving occasion, Mynt Ceremony, that night. Dr. Von Thurston refused and told him he would never amount to anything. Once an assistant, always an assistant. The next day, Evan was gone."

"And so was the coin," I add.

"And so was the coin," he repeats.

"Derek, I've got news for you: Evan works at the Crossed Palms now."

Derek's jaw drops. All he can muster is, "Oh."

Talk about a plot twist. I can't believe it. Evan was always so nice to me, making me the perfect Shirley Temple, fitting right in with the rest of the hotel staff by mastering the "look." He even got me with his signature greeting of "What's the word from the bird?" It was all a front. His nice-guy qualities were masking his strong opinions about the magicians. He never liked one magic trick, not even the innocent woven finger trap. Imagine spending all this time sabotaging the magic acts and planting these clues while serving drinks, just to get back at Dr. Von Thurston. Talk about misdirection!

"Derek, what's your father famous for? What's his gimmick?" I ask.

"He's a Renaissance man, renowned for being great in many things. But when it comes to illusions, he is untouchable," he says. "Dr. Von Thurston is famous for walking on water."

"Walking on water?!"

"Yes. To perform it, everything must go exactly as planned, which means his set must not be tinkered with. Evan, of all people, would know that. One false step can mean my father plunging into a deep pool of water."

"Waterworks instead of a magic show!" I exclaim. "We need to find Evan."

Derek hands me the coin, and I stash it with the other tokens I've accumulated. We head out to the lobby, where people are milling around. Some are about to take the remaining seats at the Great Bradinski's show. I feel a tinge of sadness. Diane is probably wondering what in the world happened to me. No one should be in the bathroom this long, but I can't risk going back to explain. We have to press on. I'll just have to make it up to her.

"Derek, I think the best thing for you would be to go back to the magic show," I say. "If Evan sees you, he will know the jig is up."

Derek refuses to listen to me. I should have known.

"I found the coin. I'm going to see this thing through."

This is what Walt would call being too close to the problem. Derek is heavily invested in making sure Evan is the guilty party. I need to do my job. And right now my job is to find out whether Evan is missing his coin. I can't ask him that with Derek tagging along.

"He won't talk if you're around. Let's compromise."

I take a slight detour to the gift shop and grab a baseball cap with the words *Crossed Palms* on it. It doesn't go with Derek's full yellow outfit, but it'll have to do.

"Keep this on. At least we can sort of obscure your face," I say. "The minute Evan is within our sights, you'll have to blend in, which seems impossible with your sunshine getup."

"I will have you know this outfit was tailor-made for me by the finest Italian designer."

If Derek were a full-time detective, he would know camouflaging is key to sleuthing. That's just basic Detective 101.

Now I have to think. Where would Evan be at this very moment? He's definitely working because earlier today he was filling the pitchers at the drink stations.

I need to speak to someone who knows the servers' schedules. Think, Goldie, think!

A server holding a tray of drinks walks with purpose across the lobby. It's Arnold! I quickly catch up to him.

"Arnold, have you seen Evan? Do you know where he's working?"

"Evan's been popping up here and there. He's scheduled right now to work at the Palms Palace. It's where I'm heading," Arnold says. "Want me to relay a message to him?"

"No thanks. I'll see you later." Arnold heads to the bar, only a few steps away, while I'm left to ponder our current predicament.

The Palms Palace is one of a few bars in the Crossed Palms Resort. It's very beautiful, with mahogany paneling throughout and wall upon wall filled with the finest wines and liquors. There are cozy little nooks where guests can sit and drink their elixirs, while others can sidle up to the long wooden bar and watch the bartenders work their magic.

I know all this because I've seen photos of the fancy bar in the hotel's brochure, enticing guests to visit. The one big caveat is that kids are not allowed inside.

"What are we waiting for?" Derek says. "Let's go."

"We can't." I point to the big ADULTS ONLY sign. "If we try, one of our security guards will kick us out in less than five minutes."

"Well, this is an emergency!"

Derek doesn't want to take my word for it, so he decides to try his luck. The minute his foot takes one step across the entrance, the doorman places his hand on Derek's chest, points to the sign, and very, very gently nudges Derek away. He walks over to me with a dejected face.

"We can't go in," he says.

I shake my head. "Tell me something I don't know!"

"What do we do now?"

We stand a little away from the bar. I don't want Evan to get even the tiniest glimpse of Derek. This is going to be tricky. Do I take up Arnold's suggestion and try to lure Evan out with a message? No, he would become too suspicious if I did that. Sneaking in is out of the question. There has to be another way.

Across the lobby I see the one person who might be willing to help our cause: The lovely Miss Dupart is heading toward the elevators. The night may be over for her. I just hope she has enough energy for one more thing.

"Stay right here and make sure our man Evan doesn't leave the bar," I say to Derek. "I'll be right back!"

I run over to Miss Dupart. I slow my steps as I draw nearer. I don't want to startle her in any way.

"Miss Dupart! Do you have a quick moment?"

She flashes her great big smile. The bracelets weighing down her wrists make clinking and clanking sounds.

"Aw, Goldie. I was just about to end my magical day a bit early," she whisper-talks. "Sometimes you must leave the party early to allow for a bit of mystery to linger."

"What would you say if I have a bit more mystery for you?" I ask. "Just a tiny bit. I'm working on a case, and I need your help."

Miss Dupart pulls in closer. "A case, you say? I do love me a thriller. It adds a little kick to the heart rate, if you know what I mean."

More jingling from her wrists. "Come with me, then."

I walk her over to Derek, who is not quite successful in blending in. The closer we get to him, the bigger Miss Dupart's eyes open.

"Now, this is quite something," she says, admiring Derek's yellow ensemble. "I live for bold sartorial choices, and this young man's stylish suit is one for the pages of *Bazaar*."

Derek turns bright red. Go figure! Who knew a compliment from Miss Dupart would stun Derek? He doesn't even pull out one of his cards!

"Miss Dupart, this is Derek Von Thurston, part-time magician, part-time detective."

"You must be the brilliant son of Dr. Von Thurston, correct? You do not have his features, but you do have his strong handshake."

If Derek turns any redder, I think he might go up in flames.

"Miss Dupart, we're in a serious bind. Because of our age, we're unable to walk into the Palms Palace," I say. "But we have to verify a particular someone."

Miss Dupart's wrinkly forehead becomes even more wrinkly.

"You two are much too young to begin imbibing.

I insist you let go of this pursuit and instead focus on other, healthier endeavors."

Derek's nervous laugh is unlike his loud cackle, which makes me think it's definitely genuine.

"We don't want to drink. We just want to see if Evan is working."

"The barman with shaggy blond hair?" Miss Dupart asks.

"Yes! That's the one," I exclaim. "The mission is this: Go inside the bar and see if Evan is there."

Miss Dupart repeats my request, just to make sure we are absolutely clear in our ask. I do need to add one more thing. I just hope Miss Dupart is up for the challenge.

"If you do see him, can you ask him about his coin?" I say. "The gold coin he's always tossing up in the air? You know the one. What do you say, Miss Dupart?"

Derek and I look at Miss Dupart with serious puppy dog eyes, the same ones she gets from her poodle, Clementine.

Puppy dog eyes, shine on!

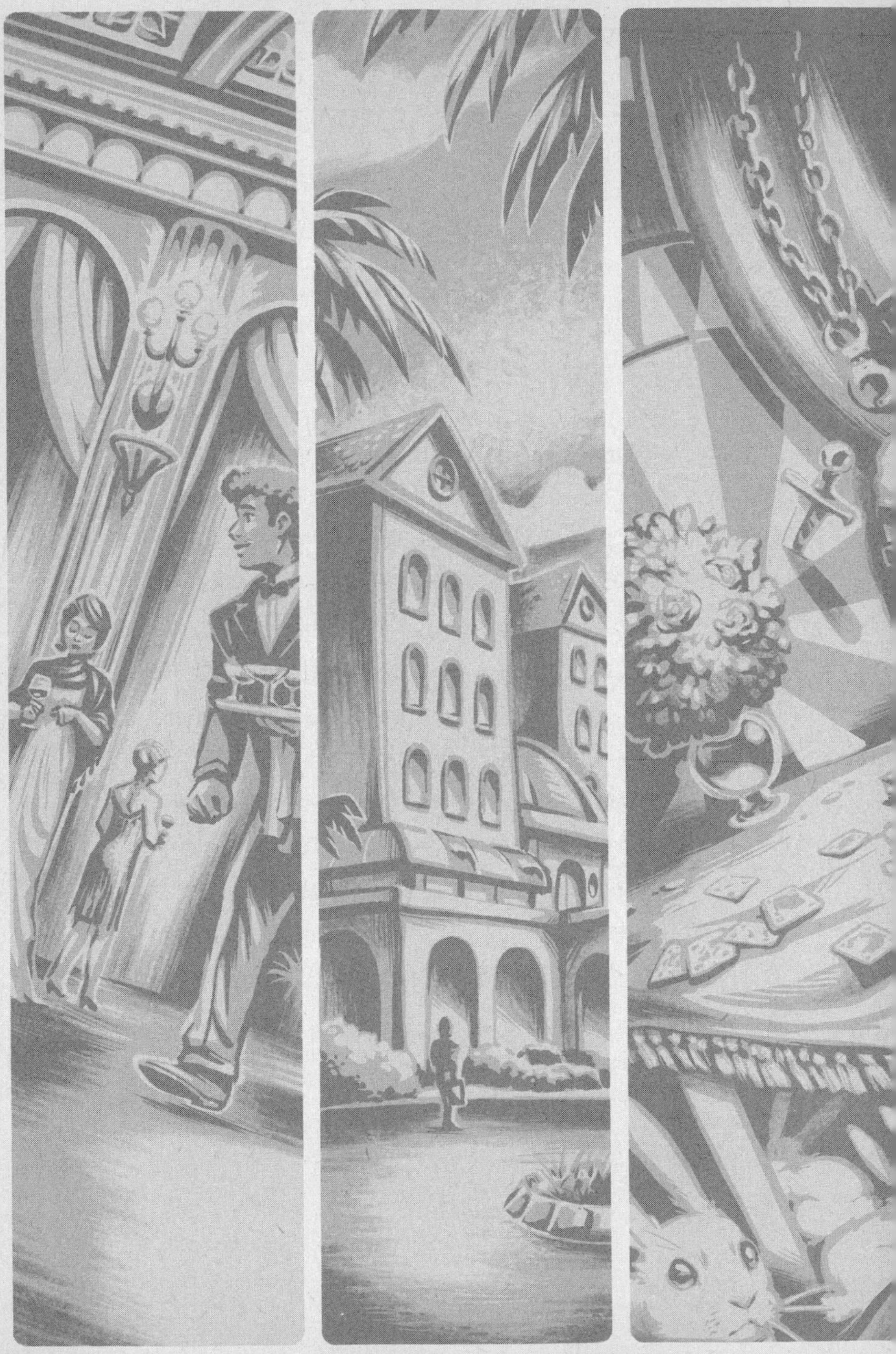

Chapter Seventeen

MISS DUPART LOOKS TO THE PALMS PALACE AND THEN back to us. Her eyes squint a bit as if she's trying to use some sort of superpower eyesight to penetrate the walls of the bar.

If only, Miss Dupart, if only.

"I have seen Evan playing with his coin on more than one occasion," she says. "It's his signature style."

"Correct!" I exclaim, and produce the coin for her to see.

"What a rare-looking coin," she says. "Is Evan missing his coin?"

"No, he stole it," Derek says. "From my father."

Miss Dupart inhales sharply.

"Thievery. How very tacky. I don't condone it in any form or manner," she whisper-talks. "A coin, no less? Material possessions are worthless unless given as a gift."

Every piece of jewelry Miss Dupart wears has a story behind it about the person who gave it to her. She cherishes each item like it's family.

"It is very tacky," Derek says.

"To bring you up to speed, I have a feeling Evan had something to do with the magic acts failing this weekend," I say. "I found this coin at the most recent act. Derek told me how Evan was his father's assistant and how the coin was given to his father, so it can't possibly be a coincidence. If the coin I found is Evan's coin, then he'll be my number one suspect."

Everything is riding on this being Evan's stolen coin. Evan's a gambling man, so I'm guessing he would be up for a little wager.

"Do you think you can find a way of asking Evan to show you his coin?" I ask. "Maybe a heads or tails bet? Get him to talk about it. What do you say, Miss Dupart?"

"A thriller it is! I would have you know, young Derek Von Thurston, that I am an accomplished thespian. From the bright lights of Broadway shows to the London West End theaters, I have embodied many,

many roles," Miss Dupart says. "I will gladly embark on the role of the unsuspecting hotel guest turned spy."

Miss Dupart walks over to the doorman, who opens the door wide enough for both Derek and me to take a quick peek in. We still can't see very well. I have to follow Miss Dupart's interactions with Evan.

"We need a better view," I say.

The Palms Palace has big glass windows that are perfect to observe through. Unfortunately, large planters overflowing with giant palm leaves practically engulf the windows, so we'll have to climb through the foliage to snoop.

I lead Derek to the potted plants and trees. Thankfully, no one is around, including the groundskeeper, who would no doubt be completely devastated if he knew what I was thinking of doing.

"We need to get in there," I say, ready to climb into the shrubbery as best I can without destroying the plant life.

"That's impossible," Derek says. "My yellow suit. It will be destroyed!"

I can't believe he's worried about his yellow suit getting dirty. Who cares about stains? When it's time to dig in the dirt to uncover the truth, you never hesitate. You simply jump right in. Derek is constantly declaring his detective prowess, yet here he is afraid.

"Derek! Don't you want to follow the action?" I ask. "I sure don't want to miss a thing."

He looks down at his yellow shoes.

"Dr. Von Thurston doesn't approve of messy appearances. Truth be told, he barely approved of my yellow suit."

I'm really starting to understand what it must be like for Derek to be a Von Thurston. Mom and Dad have never told me what I should wear. When I settled on my yellow headbands, Dad made sure to keep my drawer fully stocked. And Mom is always on the lookout for the perfect capris with deep pockets. To my parents, what matters isn't what you wear—it's how you treat others. I'm sure Dr. Von Thurston's opinion of the yellow suit is just the tip of the iceberg for Derek.

"Say no more, Derek. I'll be our eyes," I say. "You just be on the lookout. If the groundskeeper sees me in here, he'll toss me out like a pesky weed!"

I head right into the growth, placing one foot in a planter and pulling myself in. The first step is a doozy. Apparently, our fine Crossed Palms Resort staff just watered these things, so my penny loafer immediately sinks into mud.

"What do you see?" Derek asks.

I push over a couple of palm leaves until I'm able to take a clear look inside. Miss Dupart has found the perfect position, a seat directly at the center of the bar. Only one pair of guests sits with her, enjoying their drinks, so the view is pretty unobstructed. It doesn't seem as if anyone is tending to the bar. Mr. Maple would not be happy about that. Where is Evan?

Lately, I've been trying to perfect my lip-reading technique by making Cheryl and Rob have conversations far away from me while I attempt to decipher what they're saying. The first couple of times, I kept thinking Rob was asking Cheryl out on a date when he was actually asking about her birthday. It's not an exact science. Mistakes are bound to be made. But right now I'm willing to try my best.

I see Miss Dupart raise her hand, lean slightly over the bar, and say something that looks like either "too-dles" or "poodles." It can go either way. As soon as she does this, Evan pops up. He must have been kneeling down behind the bar for some reason.

Miss Dupart laughs very gaily at something Evan

has said. Evan is in the dim, moody lighting of the bar, so I can't read his lips—I just have to guess. He probably said, "What's the word from the bird?" and Miss Dupart probably laughed as if Evan were the wittiest person around.

"Nothing much is going on," I say. "Greetings and salutations. Something about a poodle, I think."

"Huh?" Derek says.

I continue to narrate. "Evan is saying *something something something* while he fills a long tumbler with ice. I think Miss Dupart is telling an interesting story, something about missions."

"Come again?" Derek says.

I'm not doing a great job. I've watched a couple of episodes of that new animal show *Wild Kingdom*. Live narration is way harder than I expected. Never underestimate the skill needed to follow the actions of a cheetah.

Evan's face suddenly turns sour, as if he's just sucked on a lemon. "Oh! She must be talking about magicians! Evan just got so angry."

Evan hands Miss Dupart her drink. As is his custom, he drops several umbrellas onto the rim of the glass. The umbrellas are definitely a cute touch. Sadly,

Miss Dupart is unable to truly sip her drink with so many of them obscuring the way.

"What's going on now?"

"Not much. Evan is tending to other guests. Miss Dupart is adjusting her rings and probably wondering how to take a sip of her drink with so many umbrellas."

"Umbrellas?"

I wonder how Miss Dupart will get him to talk about the coin. If only my detective skills included telepathy. I would beam my thoughts right into Miss Dupart's head, and she would know exactly what to do.

Evan returns. Miss Dupart says something to him. I can't make out what she's said! Darn it!

Uh-oh.

"Evan's raising his hands. He looks as if he's annoyed with Miss Dupart." He tries to hide his annoyance with a sweet smile, but his body language is a dead giveaway. He shakes his head, not once or twice but three times. Then he digs into his pocket and shows Miss Dupart something small.

"Is he really going to choose any old coin to prove his lucky coin isn't missing?" I say.

"He pulled out a coin?" Derek asks.

"He sure did."

Miss Dupart scrutinizes the coin and smiles.

"Evan flipped the coin into the palm of his hand," I say. "Miss Dupart is toasting him and finishing her drink now."

Before Miss Dupart leaves, clearly content with what she's seen, she says one more thing to Evan. I can't quite make out the words. Evan gives her a quizzical look and then drops down behind the bar, out of sight once again.

What did Miss Dupart say? And more important, what did Evan say? The suspense is killing me!

"She's coming out!" I say. I start to detangle myself from the plants. My poor penny loafers are completely covered with mud. Derek stares down at them and grimaces.

"No crying over muddy shoes," I say.

We meet Miss Dupart over by the entrance. She points to a corner where we can talk more freely. Miss Dupart really does embody the hotel guest turned spy. Thankfully, we find a table for us to sit down. I run and grab a glass of water for her. Spying can dehydrate a person.

"Miss Dupart, what happened? I couldn't lip-read the last part."

Miss Dupart takes a long sip, carefully places the glass down, and then stares deeply into our eyeballs for at least ten seconds. It's all so very dramatic, and the longer she stares, the more I feel like my eyes keep opening wider and wider.

"As we suspected, Evan was not going to be an easy riddle to solve," she says. "But he proved no match for Doriane."

"Doriane?" Both Derek and I say this at exactly the same time.

"Doriane would be my spy name, of course," she says. "My alias."

"Go on, Doriane," I say. Miss Dupart is doing us a favor, so if she wants a spy name, she gets a spy name.

"Well, the minute I mentioned how fond I was of seeing so many magicians in the vicinity, his feathers became so ruffled."

I knew she mentioned magicians!

"The real icing on the cake had to be when I asked him what my chances were of finally meeting the renowned Dr. Von Thurston," Miss Dupart says.

"You asked him about Dr. Von Thurston?" Derek says. He's not happy with Miss Dupart's line of questioning. He doesn't know Miss Dupart as I know her.

Sometimes a person's surprise reaction is all it takes to see what they are thinking and hiding. She was right to bring up Dr. Von Thurston.

"That's when he got mad," I say.

"As if right on cue," she says.

I can't imagine harboring so much anger toward one person. Yet here's Evan, carrying this outrage around like a big, heavy stone.

"It took a couple of tries to ask him about his lucky coin. Any other day he would have surely asked me heads or tails. He hesitated," she says after taking another sip. I thought watching the action while standing on a potted plant was intriguing. Hearing it from Miss Dupart adds so many more layers to it.

"Our Evan didn't want to leave anything to chance, so he finally pulled out a coin to toss up and see what my true chances were of meeting Dr. Von Thurston in person. A lifelong dream of Doriane's, of course."

"What coin did he use?" I ask.

"A bright silver quarter," she says. "I asked him where his beautiful lucky gold coin was. His response…"

Miss Dupart pauses for dramatic effect.

"He said he recently lost the coin. He said, 'I'm no longer tied to it as I once was. Sometimes the past just holds you back. You must burn the past. It's what my doctor ordered.' End quote," she says. "And scene."

Yowza. Not only did Evan admit he lost the coin but he also sort of confessed to his crimes.

"'What my doctor ordered'? He's definitely talking about Dr. Von Thurston," Derek says. "If he plans to rig my father's act, we've got to stop him."

I yank Derek's arm, preventing him from yet another attempt to get himself into the Palms Palace. We've already tried that. We need a better solution.

"Thanks, Miss Dupart, for all that you did. You are most definitely the best spy that has ever lived," I say. "After the coin toss, I wasn't able to see where Evan went."

"Our shaggy-haired server simply disappeared," Miss Dupart says in a matter-of-fact tone.

Derek and I give each other a look of astonishment. Evan did spend a lot of time with Dr. Von Thurston learning tricks. Did he actually master the art of invisibility?

"Huh?" I say, and wait with bated breath.

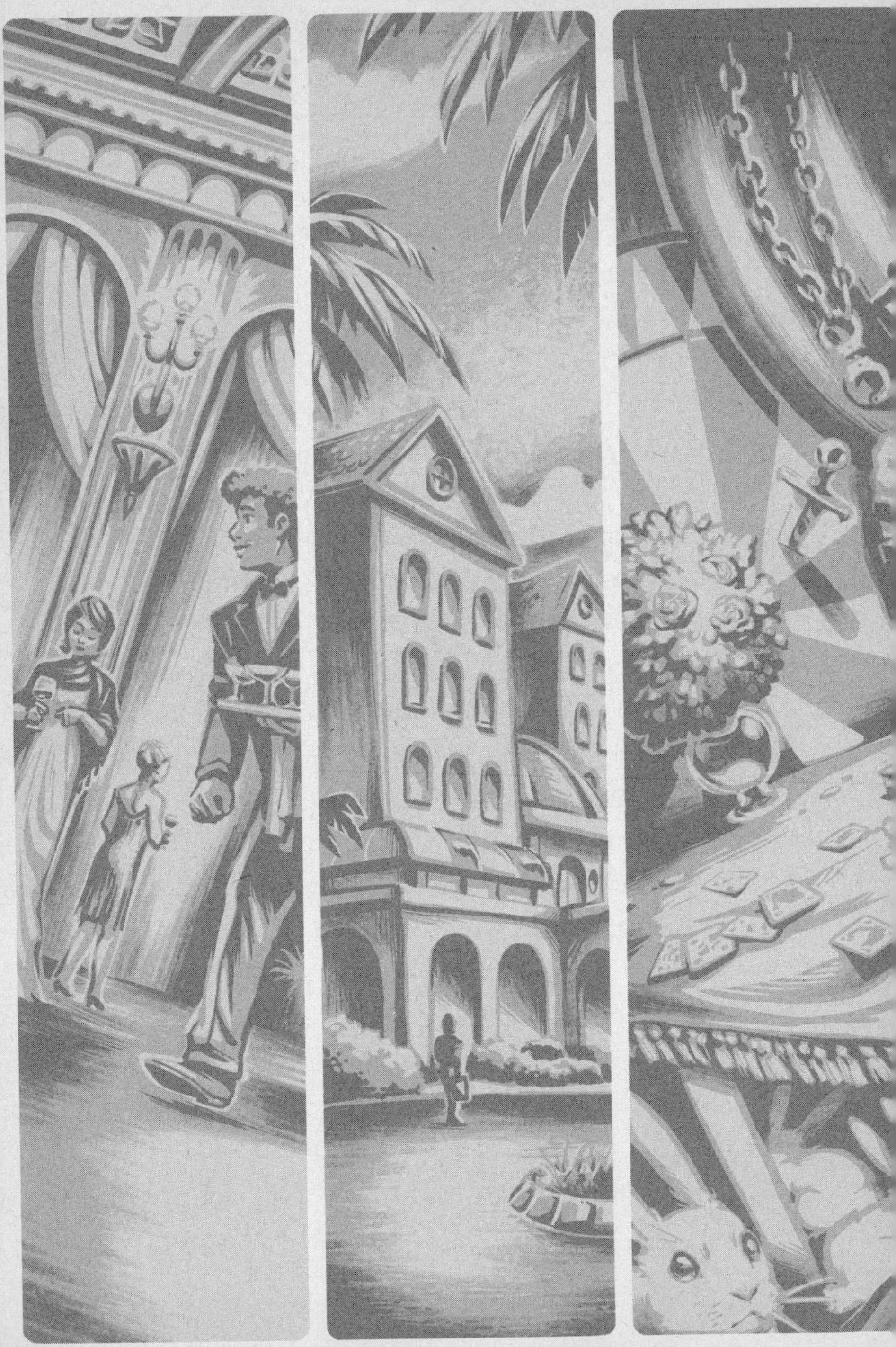

Chapter Eighteen

MISS DUPART FINISHES DRINKING HER GLASS OF WATER. She opens her purse and takes out a rather large mirror and a tube of lipstick.

"It's true," she says. "Evan went downstairs."

"Downstairs?" I ask. "What do you mean, Miss Dupart? I've seen plenty of pictures of the bar. I've never seen a set of stairs."

Miss Dupart opens the tube of lipstick and slowly lines her lips with a dusty pink color. Next, she purses them together and makes a smacking noise. Content, she puts her beauty products away.

"You two are much too young to know this, but most drinking establishments, if constructed correctly, will have a trapdoor in the floor, behind the bar," she says. "The trapdoor usually leads to where they store precious liquor or expensive wine bottles."

A trapdoor! I should have known about it. Of course, where else would Evan be dipping down into? He wasn't kneeling on the floor. He was actually leaving the bar.

"This explains so much! If there is a trapdoor, then that must mean one thing."

"That Evan is very good at stocking liquor?" Derek says sarcastically. "I could have told you that. Dr. Von Thurston always made him serve a dry martini every night."

"No, Derek, that's not it!"

I scream, but it's because I'm about to explode. This is the true break I've been waiting for. I've been racking my brain, trying to figure out how exactly Evan would be able to sneak into all these shows without anyone noticing. He set up the tea station for the Great Bradinski, and he was working the night of Angela's act, but how was he able to sabotage the other acts? The trapdoor explains everything.

"The trapdoor most definitely leads to the tunnels underneath the Crossed Palms Resort," I say. "It's practically a whole other universe down there."

Derek is finally getting my meaning. "It makes perfect sense. He would be able to visit where these magicians were storing their tricks before hitting the stage," he says.

"Exactly! Plus, the bunnies!" I exclaim. "Evan must have stored the bunnies somewhere underground. I'm sure of it."

"We need to bring this to the authorities," Derek says.

I can't believe Derek wants to go to the cops instead of just solving the mystery first. Right now we need to stop Evan while we're hot on his tail. Alerting others will only delay us.

Miss Dupart places her hand softly over Derek's shoulder. Derek is taken aback by the warm gesture. It seems as if he's not used to such genuine expressions.

"Derek, you seem to be very attuned to many things. You clearly have a sense of style. You're a young man who is not afraid to make bold choices," she says. "I've met many such men. I've also known them to take necessary precautions when faced with adversity. You put your trousers on one leg at a time. You analyze and think through your ensemble."

Derek nods. He's really listening to what Miss Dupart is saying. It's kind of a miracle.

"Wouldn't you agree the best solution would be to

prove your findings before taking them to the men in uniform?"

Derek pauses for a long minute. "I think you're right," he says timidly.

I pat him hard on his back. *Of course I'm right! I'm a great house detective, and this mystery is about to get solved*, I think.

I give Miss Dupart the biggest hug ever. She's been so helpful! Without her, we would have never caught this break.

"Thank you for everything, Miss Dupart. I owe you a cherry Coke or two!" I say. "Actually, I'd be more than happy to take Clementine for her morning walks for a week."

"You are very welcome. It was a great, unexpected nightcap. *And* I was able to bring forth Doriane for a one-act play," she says. "On that note, I bid you both a good and productive night of sleuthing."

Miss Dupart stands up and heads to the elevator. It's time for us to pick up the pieces and find the right entrance to the underground. I have to think this one through.

"I probably should be heading out, too," Derek says.

What? I'm so confused. Hasn't Derek been by my side ever since we met yesterday? Didn't he insist on telling me how he was a detective? This doesn't make sense.

"Why?" I ask.

"Because it's obvious I'm nothing more than a part-time detective," he says. "If I were a *true* detective, I would have thrown myself into the planters with you. Or figured out that Evan was the culprit. Instead, I've just been in the way. The only helpful thing I did was name our mystery: the Case of the Missing Props."

"It's true we haven't seen eye to eye since we've met, and we might not see eye to eye in the next five minutes," I say. "But you did help me figure out this case. If you hadn't shared the information about Evan and the Swedish coin, I never would have pieced it together."

As much as Derek annoys me, he *did* help. But I disagree wholeheartedly with him. The Case of the Missing Props is way too on the nose and lacking a certain magical flair to be the name of this case.

"Let's head underground and see what we can find. Two sets of eyes are always better than one."

"Okay, I'm in." He pulls the cap farther down his head and tucks in his yellow shirt. "Where to?"

That's a good question. I'm not exactly sure. Since Derek is now officially with me, I can't possibly head to the women's bathroom and go through the entrance I used earlier. I'll have to locate another entrance—one that won't draw any attention.

"Let me think," I say, scratching the back of my yellow headband.

I absentmindedly watch Arnold leave the Palms Palace with a tray of half-eaten food. He quickly walks over to one of the hotel's restaurants, right next to the Palace.

"I got it!" I say. "Follow me."

We duck down a bit as we pass the Palms Palace, just in case Evan decides to pop up again from the trapdoor. I go into the restaurant and say hello to the host. She waves back. I always believe in walking with purpose, because that way no one can question what you are doing or why.

With Derek right behind me, we head toward the kitchen. Not all the guests at the hotel this weekend are part of the magic convention, so quite a few tables are taken up with people waiting for their meals.

The first person I see when I go through the swinging kitchen door is Chef François. He is much too busy dealing with the late dinner rush to pay attention to what I'm doing. He yells out instructions for the line cooks, and boy, are they following his orders.

With all the hustle and bustle happening, I easily lead Derek to the pantry in the back of the kitchen. No one pays us any mind. It's filled with the usual items you would find in a pantry, all neatly organized in their categories. Racks upon racks of spices, towers of vegetables, bottles of olive oil. The restaurant is never lacking.

"Here we are," I say, showing Derek the pantry.

"What do rows of paprika have to do with underground hotel tunnels?" he asks, scrutinizing the food. "Great for adding flavor, not for finding missing Chakra Cards."

Oh, ye of little faith!

"You're failing to see what is right before your eyes." I stand in front of a tall silver shelf brimming with labeled vegetables. So much good stuff here: artichokes, bunches of arugula, bok choy. Chef François keeps this shelf up-to-date with the freshest finds from the hotel garden and local farmers. "This shelf is Chef François's pride and joy. He spends every day tending to his garden and selecting the finest vegetables.

Chef François also likes to roll his ingredients around. Which is why I can do this."

I push the shelf aside very easily to reveal a concealed trapdoor. "See?"

"Excellent!"

"We better be quick. One of the cooks is bound to come back here for vegetable oil or something."

Derek opens the trapdoor and we look down. It's pretty dark.

"After you," Derek says. "You seem to know your way around."

Before I head into the darkness, I do one more thing: I steal carrots from the pantry and hand them to Derek. "For Esme, Coco, and Snowball."

Derek stores the carrots in the front pocket of his yellow suit jacket without questioning. Score one to me for converting him into my own assistant detective!

We quickly climb down the ladder, and I make sure the door closes behind us. We reach the bottom in no time.

"This is the tricky part," I whisper to Derek. I point to the long corridor to our left. "Right down there is where we'll surely find the trapdoor that Evan uses to exit the Palms Palace. We can walk toward it, but we have to be extra quiet. He could be anywhere. We can't let him see or hear us. Understood?"

"Understood."

I press my body against the wall of the corridor. Derek tries to follow, but he's nervous he might stain his suit. Everything is grimy. Dusty pipes hang over our heads. Boxes and abandoned machinery litter the halls. These tunnels are the keepers of lost and forgotten items.

I have my nifty flashlight. I carry it with me at all times so I can easily shine a light on a situation that calls for it, but I'd rather not use it right now. We need to find out if Evan's down here, and I don't want to alert him to our whereabouts. Even though Derek and I stay light on our feet, every single step we take seems to echo across the corridors. There are other strange acoustics. Dripping sounds. Hard stomps from above. The thrumming bass of a drum.

"What's that?" Derek asks.

I stop in my tracks. I, too, hear a strange noise. It sounds like thumping. It could very well be the pipes. I can't be sure, not from this distance.

"Let's keep going," I say.

We tiptoe along the dark, spooky corridor until I

stop right underneath what should be the Palms Palace. The trapdoor is shut. I shine my flashlight for just a quick minute to reveal what I suspected: footprints! There's only one set of footprints heading down the unlit corridor toward the thumping sound.

Right beside the footprints is a thin rope. It seems fairly new because there's no dust on it. Next to it are three gallons of gasoline. Is Evan planning to dump the gasoline in the pool of water Dr. Von Thurston is going to walk on? Evan's plans are way worse than I could have ever imagined! I do the smart thing and carefully drag the gasoline away from the trapdoor, only to find out one of the gallons is empty! I can only hope we'll be able to stop Evan before something really bad happens!

I hoist the rope over my shoulder. This might come in handy.

I turn to Derek and point in the direction we'll be walking next. Then I press my finger against my lips, the universal sign to keep quiet. I hope Derek listens because this is super important. I want to avoid any surprises. To be extra careful, I even take my loafers off and point to Derek's yellow shoes. He shakes his head. I nod like I'm a pigeon. Eventually, he relents and takes them off. We simply can't risk blowing our cover.

My toes curl up as soon as I take my first step. Dark and now cold!

Evan had better be down here, and we'd better find him before my poor toes freeze!

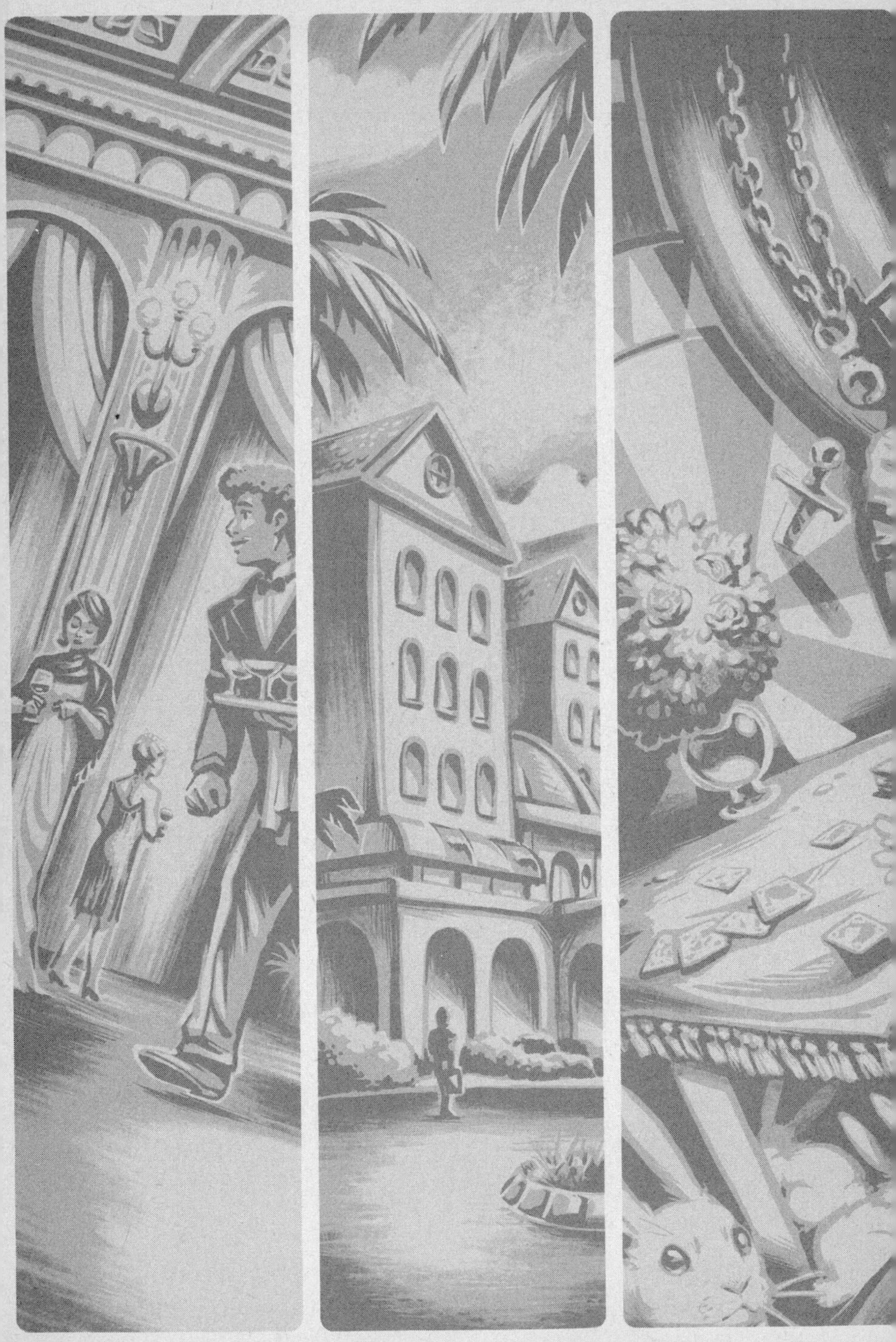

Chapter Nineteen

THE COLD IS GETTING TO DEREK AS WELL. I CAN TOTALLY hear his teeth chattering. The thumping sound is becoming louder and louder with each step. The amount of stuff "stored" down here keeps increasing to the point that we have to be extra careful not to stub our now-bare toes.

I see a very dim light at the far end of the corridor. Strange how, in the dark, your peepers search for a luminous glow like a moth. My legs find their courage to continue and so does Derek.

When the light becomes slightly brighter, we slow down but keep inching closer and closer. The light emanates from a door left ajar.

"Look, you three. I got you some water. I don't have time to get you food, too."

Evan! As soon as we hear his voice, I stop moving. A dresser covered in the thickest layer of dust is located across from the door. I drop to the ground and make myself real acquainted with the floor.

To my surprise, Derek does the same. His yellow suit will never recover! I'm used to playing in the dirt. There are tons of pictures documenting my adventures in soil and muck. You can't be too worried about appearances when you are sleuthing. Plus, my outfit has mud caked on it from my stakeout in the planters. One more stain won't change anything for me. Poor Derek. His yellow suit is toast.

We crouch down behind the dresser. In the shadowy hallway, Evan can't possibly see us, but his bright blond hair practically glows from what little light is emanating from the room. Because it's so deathly quiet, his voice reverberates against the walls. He sounds like a big old giant, and I have to remind myself: This is the same shaggy-blond-haired guy who poured me hundreds of Shirley Temples. He's no giant.

"Be quiet!" Evan says.

I finally realize what the sound is—distressed bunnies thumping their feet! Poor Coco, Esme, and Snowball! They must be so scared. It only gets worse, causing Evan to tell them to shut up again. Now I'm the one getting angry. Why would anyone scream at innocent bunnies? Did Evan not watch Bugs Bunny cartoons when he was a kid? What a terrible injustice. I won't stand for this much longer.

"I never thought I would be hiding bunnies underneath a luxury hotel," Evan says. "Then again, I thought I was going to be a world-famous magician by now. I would have been one if it weren't for Dr. Von Selfish."

Derek inhales angrily and I almost faint. Any sudden noise and we're bound to get caught. Thankfully, Evan is too into speaking to the bunnies to pay attention to how Derek wants to pound his face in. Funny how Evan goes on and on about how Dr. Von Thurston is greedy and a narcissist, yet he can't stop talking about himself and the way he was treated.

He continues: "You know, Dr. Von Thurston said I would never amount to anything and I didn't have any real talent. He was so wrong. The only thing left is to finish dumping the rest of the gasoline. A flash paper tossed at the precise moment, and boom, no more calls for Dr. Von Thurston. Isn't that right, you annoying furry rodents?"

Derek elbows me so hard I almost lose my balance.

He's feeling the rage as much as I am, maybe more so. Whatever issues he may have with his father, of course Derek still loves him. Why else would he be risking his father's sartorial wrath to protect him from Evan's diabolical plan?

"Well, drink up. I need to head back upstairs. Time to set up the grand ballroom for tomorrow," Evan says. "The doctor will not know what hit him."

When he says the word *grand,* he uses air quotes, which is very strange since the bunnies surely don't understand how air quotes work.

We can't let Evan leave the room. But how can we stop him? Time's up. I need to make a move before he does. I give Derek one last look, and he stares back at me in fear. I tiptoe and stand right by the open door.

"Okay, in you go," Evan says. I hear the sound of a scuffle. Then, "Hey, get back here!"

One of the rabbits makes a run for it, and I feel a rush of exhilaration. Could Snowball or Coco be trying to hop toward freedom? The rabbit leaps into a dark corner, and Evan panics. While he's preoccupied, I take a good look around the room. It's filled with abandoned hotel furniture. Evan was about to store the bunnies in a chest of drawers, but Freedom Bunny wasn't about to allow that to happen, not without a fight.

"I don't have time for this. Where are you?"

The rabbit makes a beeline to a large linen closet. The closet has a small hole in the corner, just big enough for the bunny to slip right through.

"Oh no, you're not about to live in luxury in this closet," Evan says. "You belong with your siblings in solitary confinement."

Evan opens the linen closet and leans in. His whole body is practically inside. He tries to grab ahold of the rabbit, but Freedom Bunny is much too quick. Unable to get a firm grip, Evan steps into the closet.

"There you are!" Evan says.

With not a second to lose, I sneak behind him, push him right into the closet, and slam the door shut!

"Hurry!" I scream at Derek, and he throws himself atop the linen closet. Evan is kicking at the door, almost lifting it open, but Derek proves to be way stronger than he looks.

"Quick. Do something!" Derek yells. "He's about to bust through."

"Not if I can help it!"

I grab the rope I snatched earlier and put it to good use. I start to tie it around the closet, circling it a few times. I create several elaborate knots as quickly as possible. There's more than enough rope to keep the closet doors shut. More than enough to keep our dis-gruntled Evan secured in one spot until we're able to alert Walt and Mr. Maple to all his misdeeds.

"Whoever is doing this, I demand you release me," Evan screams. "I work here, so you are going to be in big trouble."

Derek knocks on the closet. "Actually, Evan, the only person who is in big trouble is you."

"Derek Von Thurston? Is that you? Hey, kid, what's the word?" he says, trying to sound as calm as possible, but there's no denying the crack in his voice. "Derek, hey, remember how I used to take care of you? I prom-ise I'll explain everything if you'll just open this up. We go way back. What do you say?"

"Evan was your babysitter?" I ask. I can't imagine Derek as a little kid. He must have been constantly reciting long speeches for all to hear.

"Evan wasn't very good at taking care of me. I vividly remember I was on my own for the most part while he devoured Dr. Von Thurston's books on magic. I guess I didn't mind it because he always made me such elaborate drinks."

"Shirley Temples?" I ask, and Derek nods. Boy, Evan's Shirley Temples are world-famous!

Evan pounds on the door some more. "Who's with you? Is that Goldie? Goldie, get me out of here! This isn't funny."

I walk over to the closet. "I think you should've forgotten about the magic thing, Evan. Drinks are where your skills truly shine. Too bad you couldn't see that."

Evan responds by kicking the linen closet some more. The closet is old and made from sturdy wood. He won't be escaping anytime soon.

A bundle of white fur slowly emerges from under the closet. Freedom Bunny! Derek jumps from atop the closet and bends down to greet the bunny. For whatever reason, it hops right into his open arms.

"Hey, little one. Are you hungry?" Derek asks. He pulls out a carrot and the bunny flashes a big grin. Well, I don't know if bunnies can actually smile, but this one certainly seems happy to be free of Evan.

We locate the other two bunnies and feed them nice, fresh carrots as well. They are starving. Poor little ones.

"Well, look at that!"

Right beside the bunnies are the keys to the Great Bradinski's straitjackets, a deck of Chakra Cards, a large stack of flash papers, and finally, Angela's silver linking ring.

"Let's bring these cuties up for air," I say, nuzzling the one I think is Coco. She has long streaks of black on her eyes, like she's wearing mascara.

"Aren't you worried he might break out?" Derek asks. Evan is still banging on the closet. He's now added cursing to his repertoire.

"He's not going anywhere," I say. "The rope trick I administered is called the constrictor. I also added a bowline knot, which features the rabbit hole. I can go on about knots! I learned them all from a couple of Boy Scouts!"

I think I'm starting to sound a little like Derek, going on and on about knots.

"Wow, Goldie, you're not bad for a house detective slash car valet," Derek says, juggling two bunnies against his yellow suit jacket.

"Not bad? I'm the best!"

It's true. I am.

"Hi, Coco, Esme, or Snowball. My name is Goldie!" I say, and use my flashlight to illuminate our path back.

Chapter Twenty

I'VE NEVER BEEN ONE FOR ICED TEA. I'VE ALWAYS BEEN a water girl. However, this iced tea is made with some amazing ingredients, including mint and raspberries. I grab a pitcher and make sure to refill the glasses at our table.

"Would you like some more?" I ask.

"Thanks, Goldie," Diane says.

Diane. I had to explain a lot. I *did* abandon her at the Great Bradinski's show. She understood why. Still, no one likes to be stood up, especially for work. She responded with the sweetest thing. She said, "It's not work if you love doing it. And you love it, don't you? I would never get in the way of something you like."

Isn't she peachy?

I pour a glass of iced tea for Rob and then another for Cheryl.

"These are the best seats in the house!" Rob declares. "How were you able to score them? The show has been sold out for months."

We are seated at the closest table to the stage. In a few minutes, Dr. Von Thurston will be closing out this year's League of Magical Arts Convention. The ballroom is packed. Not an empty seat to be had.

"I happen to know the right people," I say.

The fancy front-row table is courtesy of Dr. Von Thurston and Derek. I received a card with the invitation. The card had my name embossed in gold, and it said I could invite four people to the table. It was a total no-brainer to ask Diane, Cheryl, and Rob.

"No more for me or Clementine," Miss Dupart says. She pats Clementine, who seems just as excited as we are for the show to begin. Miss Dupart is the fifth person at our table. I'm so glad everyone said yes when I asked if they would like to join me! It was the least I could do.

When Derek and I climbed up the trapdoor and into Chef François's kitchen, we caused quite the uproar. It's not very sanitary to have live animals in the kitchen. Chef François started screaming in French. Sadly, I knew the words he said all too well.

That was our first hurdle. The next came soon after we located Walt. We needed to make sure Evan was taken into custody. I was confident in my rope-tying skills, but you never know. Evan may have read a chapter or two on escapology. I didn't want to take any chances, so we rushed off. He was standing in the back of the ballroom, surveying the situation while the Great Bradinski performed.

"Walt! Evan is our man. We caught him!" I screamed right into the ballroom, which was probably not the best way to convey information. The whole audience turned around and gasped in unison. Poor Bradinski. His show was destined to be interrupted no matter what.

"What are you talking about?" Walt asked as he eyed the rabbits.

"It was Evan the bartender all along," I said.

Derek concurred. "He used to be Dr. Von Thurston's assistant. He didn't leave with a job recommendation, I will tell you that."

I showed Walt the gold coin and all the other pieces of evidence we found. He couldn't believe it. Neither could Dr. Von Thurston, who just so happened to be in the audience for the Great Bradinski's performance. Derek was wrong about his father ditching the show. I guess it never hurts to always be watching what your competition is doing.

"What is the meaning of all this?" Dr. Von Thurston demanded. He approached us, directing a stern look of disappointment to Derek. "And what happened to your suit?"

"Dad—I mean, Dr. Von Thurston. I can explain." Derek stumbled over his words. Lucky for him, he still had Freedom Bunny snuggled in his arms, and I think that calmed him.

I took a step right up to his father.

"Dr. Von Thurston, Derek and I have just cracked open the Case of the Missing Props. We've located the culprit and apprehended him," I said. "If it weren't for Derek and his mutual desire for justice, we would not have been able to secure the release of Esme, Snowball, and Coco."

Dr. Von Thurston never raised his voice. Instead, he spoke even quieter. I could barely make out what he said to his son.

"Is this true?"

Derek hesitated but eventually nodded. "Yes, Dr. Von Thurston. What Goldie said is all true."

Dr. Von Thurston bowed his head slightly and turned to Walt. "Of course my son would solve this mystery," he said. "The Von Thurstons are always on the case."

I'm almost sure my eyebrows flew straight up to my scalp after listening to his declaration. I was just about to explain what happened when Derek stepped up to the plate.

"Actually, Dr. Von Thurston, it was all Goldie. I was just assisting her."

Dr. Von Thurston's face was a wall of confusion. I guess he wasn't used to a Von Thurston playing second fiddle to anyone. Ha!

"This is a treat from table two." I flash back to the present as Arnold, our server, places a large vanilla cake in the center of the table and starts cutting pieces. I look over at table two and see Serge, aka Sir Thomas Browne, who waves at us. When we finally reunited him with his bunnies, he couldn't stop crying, which made me cry with happiness. Those bunnies were so happy to see Serge. They kept hopping about and landing on his lap. Chef François sent up a crate

227

full of fresh vegetables from his garden for them. Now the rabbits are resting and eating like the Crossed Palms Resort guests they were meant to be.

"Chocolate cake!" exclaims Cheryl.

I'm so glad Cheryl and Rob didn't have to work today. We were all given another day off. And now we can enjoy the show.

I get up and take a large slice of the cake. "Hey, Arnold. Do you mind sending this piece over to table five?"

"Not a problem, Goldie."

"Who's at table five?" Diane asks.

"The Great Bradinski and his talented assistant, Penelope. I figured they might like something sweet before the show."

Because of yesterday's turmoil, Mr. Maple came up with a solution that made sense. The Great Bradinski was asked to perform today during a special lunch catered by the Crossed Palms Resort for all the convention attendees to enjoy for free. I finally got to see the Great Bradinski escape from a locked straitjacket. The funny thing is that although I know exactly how the trick is performed, I was still shocked when he escaped before time ran out.

That's the beauty of magic. If you just suspend disbelief for a moment, you can really enjoy yourself. Not quite an easy task for a detective like me, but I'm willing to give magic another try. Instead of trying to figure out how they do the trick, I'll just take in the enchantment.

A boy dressed in a bright-red suit is making his way across the Sugar Maple Ballroom. Red is definitely Derek's color. The dramatic hue complements his dark-brown hair. He turns to our table, gives a polite wave, and sits down in the best seat in the house.

After returning the rescued bunnies and stolen props to their rightful owners, Derek and I were eager to rest. We were both exhausted and didn't have much to say, which is rare for me and even rarer for him.

Just when he was about to head toward the elevator, Derek stopped and extended his hand for a shake.

Just when he was about
to head toward the
elevator, Derek stopped
and extended his hand
for a shake.

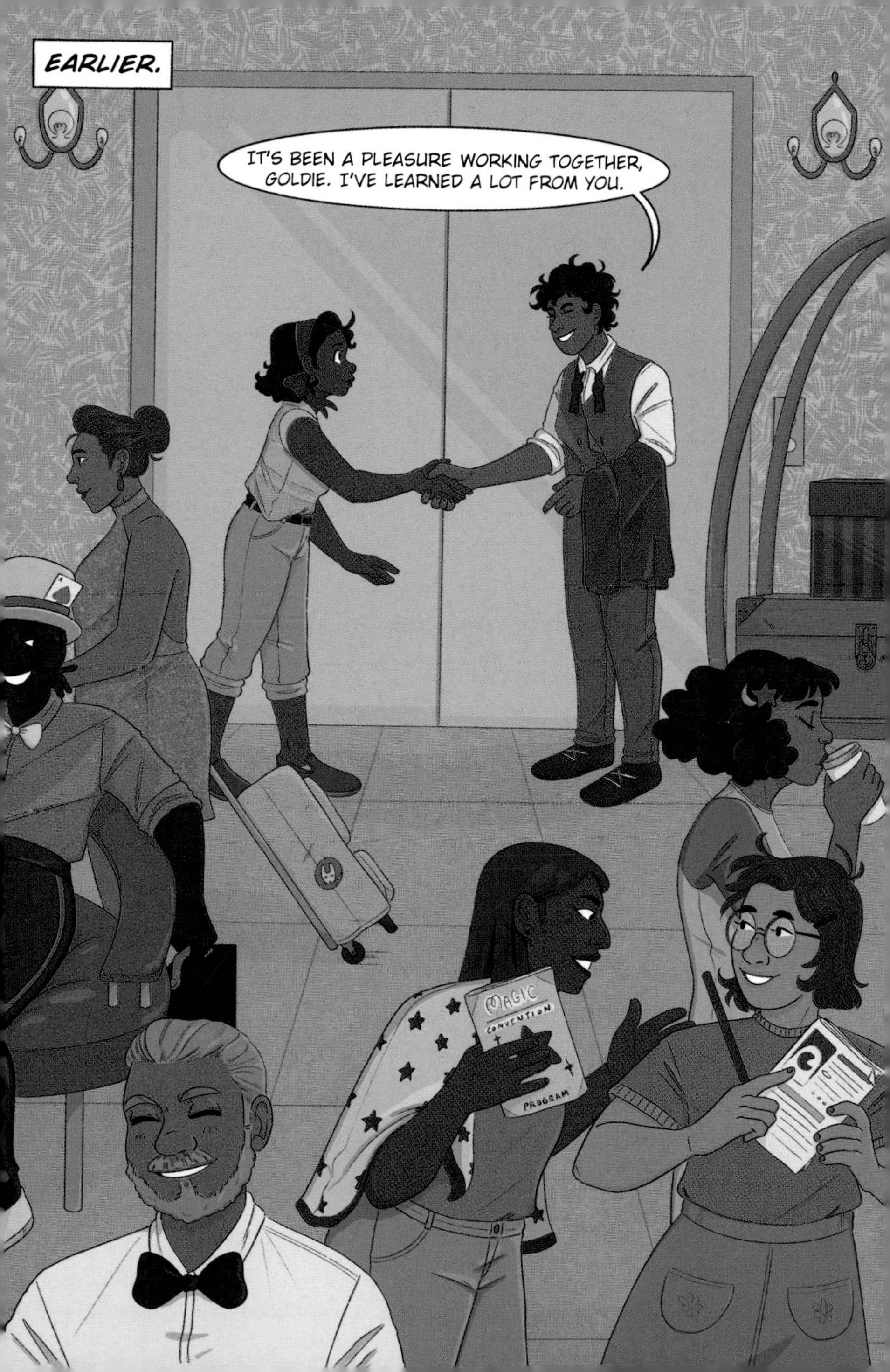
EARLIER.
IT'S BEEN A PLEASURE WORKING TOGETHER, GOLDIE. I'VE LEARNED A LOT FROM YOU.
MAGIC CONVENTION PROGRAM

IT WAS A GAS, DEREK VON THURSTON! I'M ALWAYS HAPPY TO SHARE MY SLEUTHING SKILLS WITH AN UP-AND-COMER.

SEE YOU AROUND, DEREK, AND GOOD LUCK WITH YOUR MAGICIAN LIFE.

GOOD LUCK WITH YOUR DETECTIVE LIFE. CROSSED PALMS IS LUCKY TO HAVE YOU.

SEE YA AROUND!

SWISH

CLICK!

I'M ACTUALLY GOING TO MISS THAT COOL HEAD AND HIS COLORFUL THREADS.

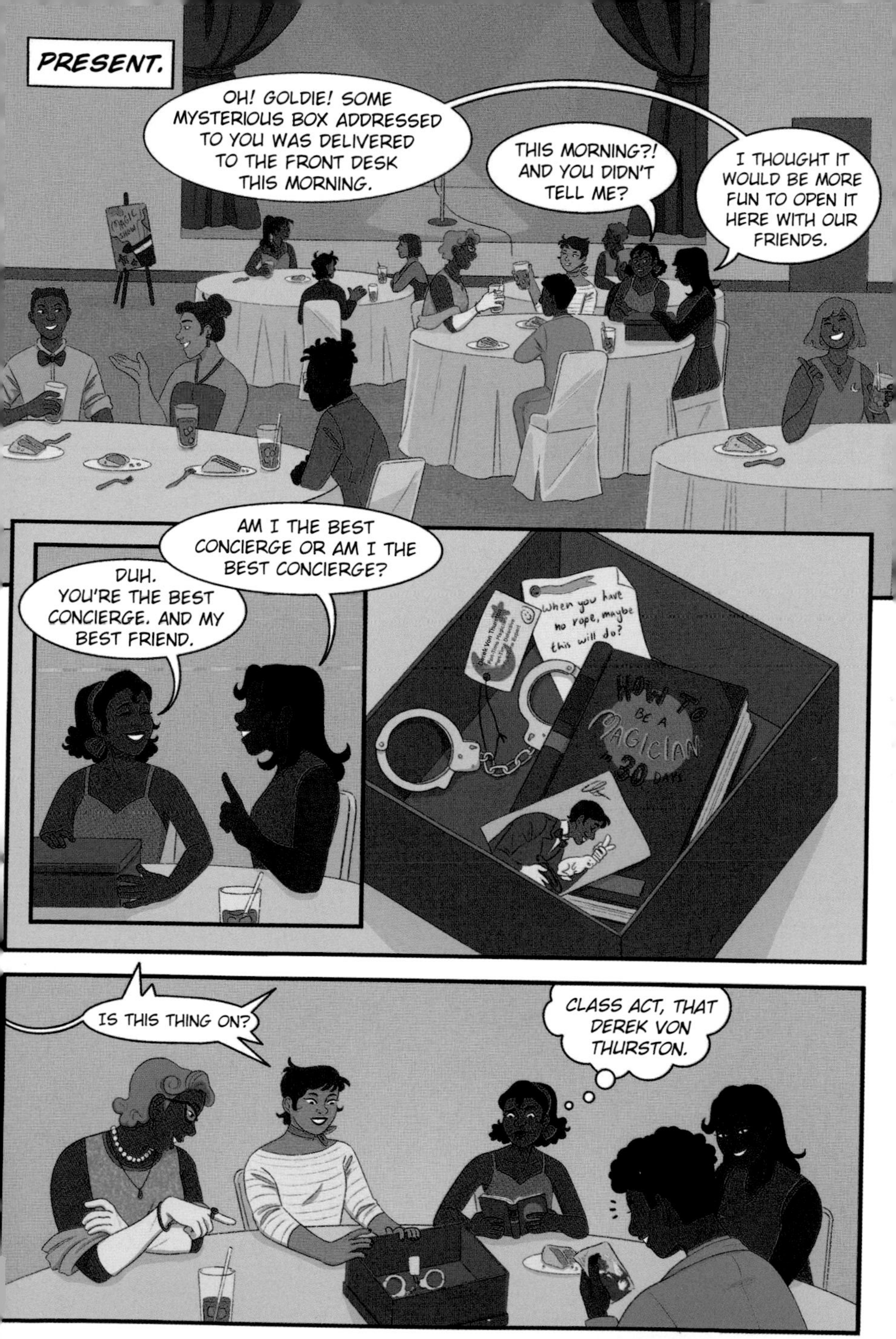
PRESENT.
MAGIC SHOW
OH! GOLDIE! SOME MYSTERIOUS BOX ADDRESSED TO YOU WAS DELIVERED TO THE FRONT DESK THIS MORNING.
THIS MORNING?! AND YOU DIDN'T TELL ME?
I THOUGHT IT WOULD BE MORE FUN TO OPEN IT HERE WITH OUR FRIENDS.
AM I THE BEST CONCIERGE OR AM I THE BEST CONCIERGE?
DUH. YOU'RE THE BEST CONCIERGE. AND MY BEST FRIEND.
When you have no rope, maybe this will do?
HOW TO BE A MAGICIAN in 30 DAYS
IS THIS THING ON?
CLASS ACT, THAT DEREK VON THURSTON.

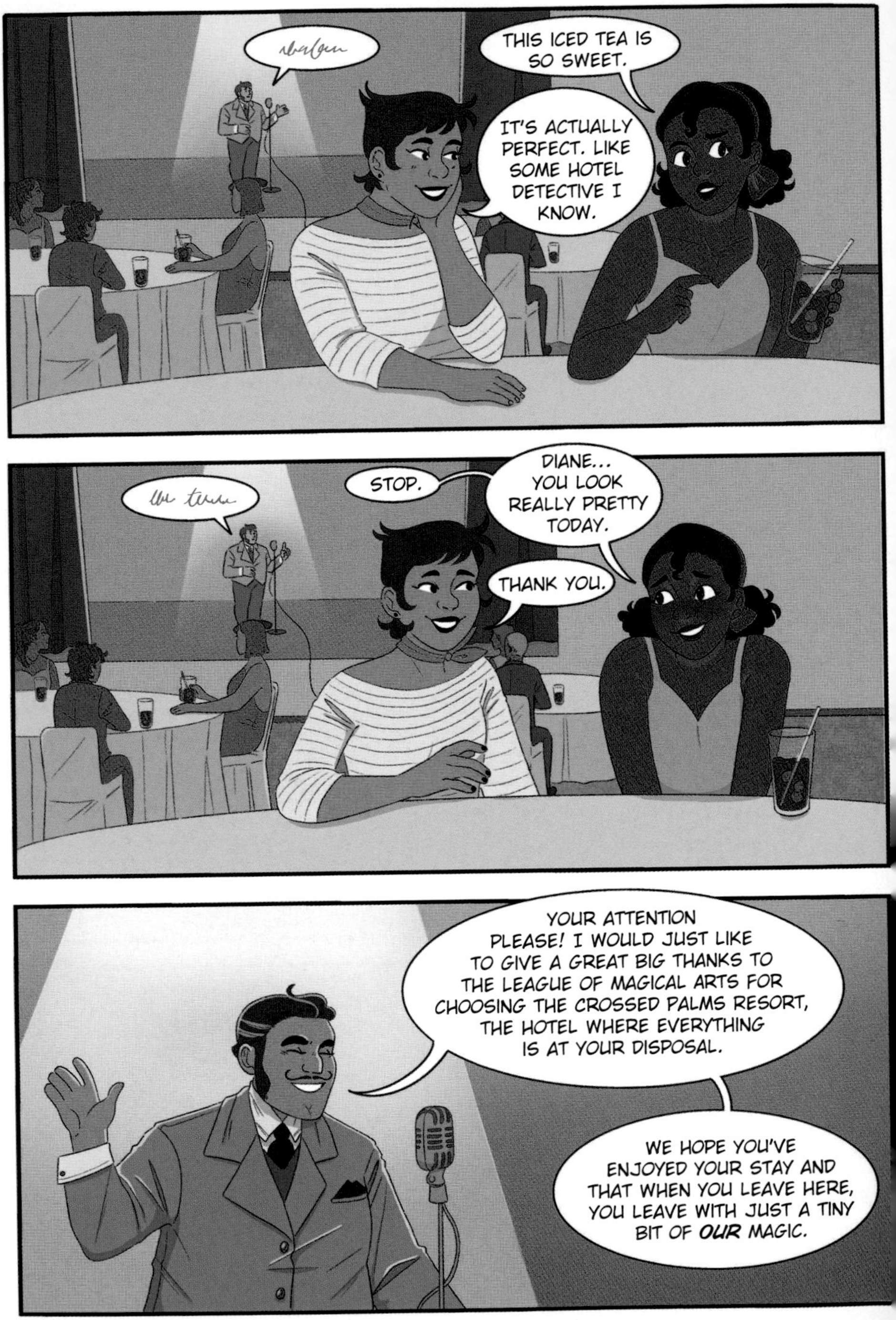
THIS ICED TEA IS SO SWEET.
IT'S ACTUALLY PERFECT. LIKE SOME HOTEL DETECTIVE I KNOW.
DIANE... YOU LOOK REALLY PRETTY TODAY.
STOP.
THANK YOU.
YOUR ATTENTION PLEASE! I WOULD JUST LIKE TO GIVE A GREAT BIG THANKS TO THE LEAGUE OF MAGICAL ARTS FOR CHOOSING THE CROSSED PALMS RESORT, THE HOTEL WHERE EVERYTHING IS AT YOUR DISPOSAL.
WE HOPE YOU'VE ENJOYED YOUR STAY AND THAT WHEN YOU LEAVE HERE, YOU LEAVE WITH JUST A TINY BIT OF ***OUR*** MAGIC.

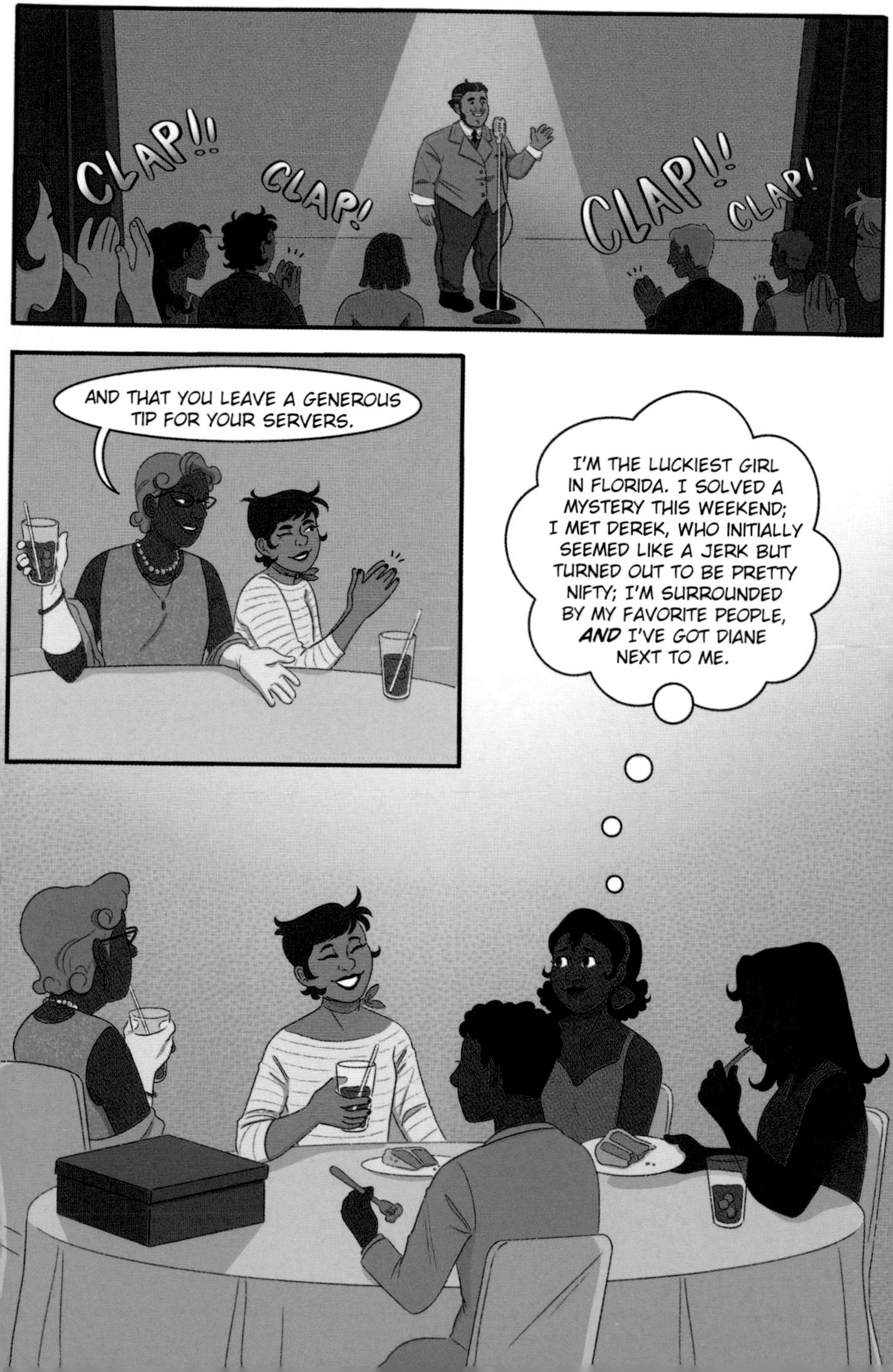
CLAP!!
CLAP!
CLAP!!
CLAP!
AND THAT YOU LEAVE A GENEROUS TIP FOR YOUR SERVERS.
I'M THE LUCKIEST GIRL IN FLORIDA. I SOLVED A MYSTERY THIS WEEKEND; I MET DEREK, WHO INITIALLY SEEMED LIKE A JERK BUT TURNED OUT TO BE PRETTY NIFTY; I'M SURROUNDED BY MY FAVORITE PEOPLE, AND I'VE GOT DIANE NEXT TO ME.

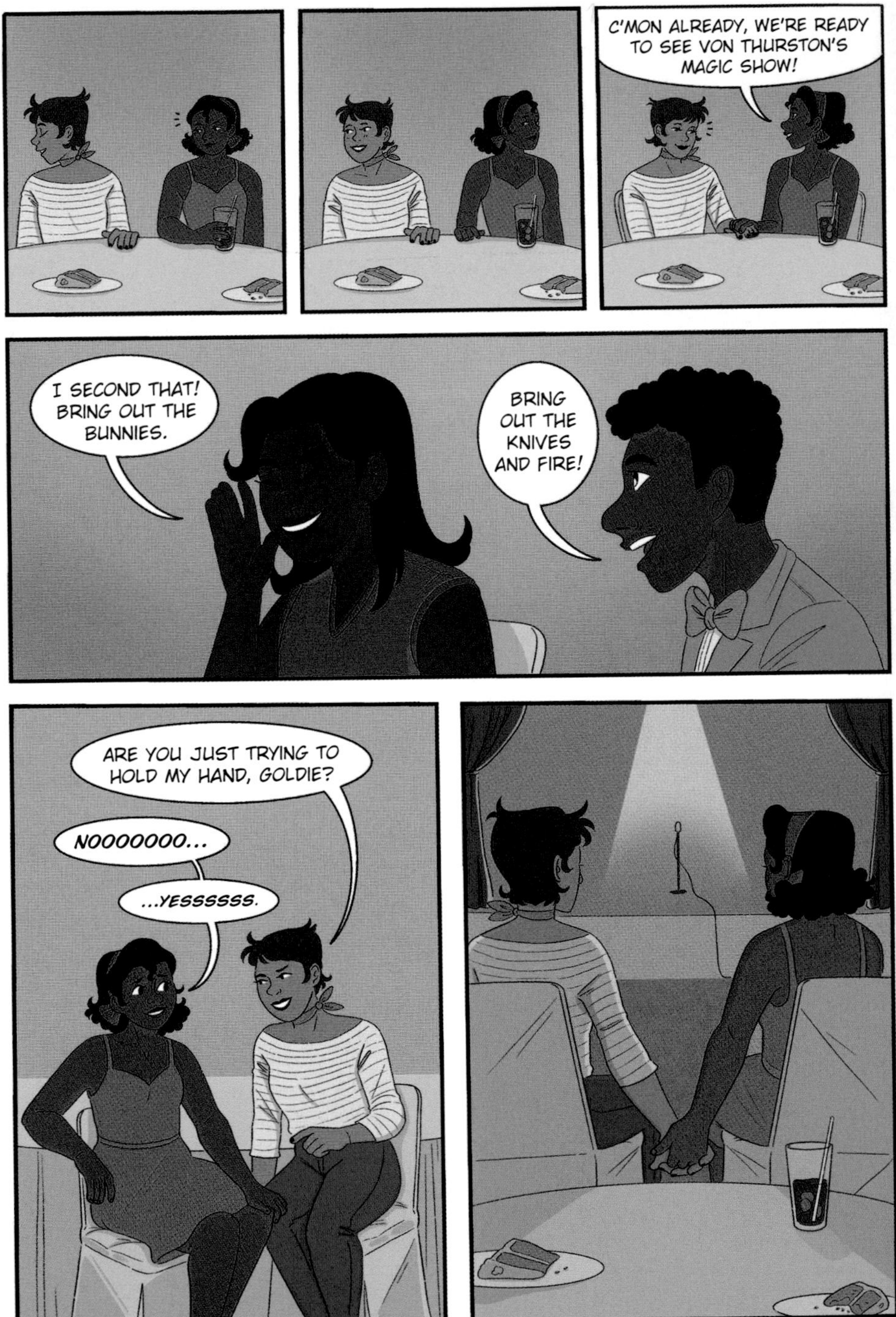
C'MON ALREADY, WE'RE READY TO SEE VON THURSTON'S MAGIC SHOW!
I SECOND THAT! BRING OUT THE BUNNIES.
BRING OUT THE KNIVES AND FIRE!
ARE YOU JUST TRYING TO HOLD MY HAND, GOLDIE?
NOOOOOOO...
...YESSSSSS.

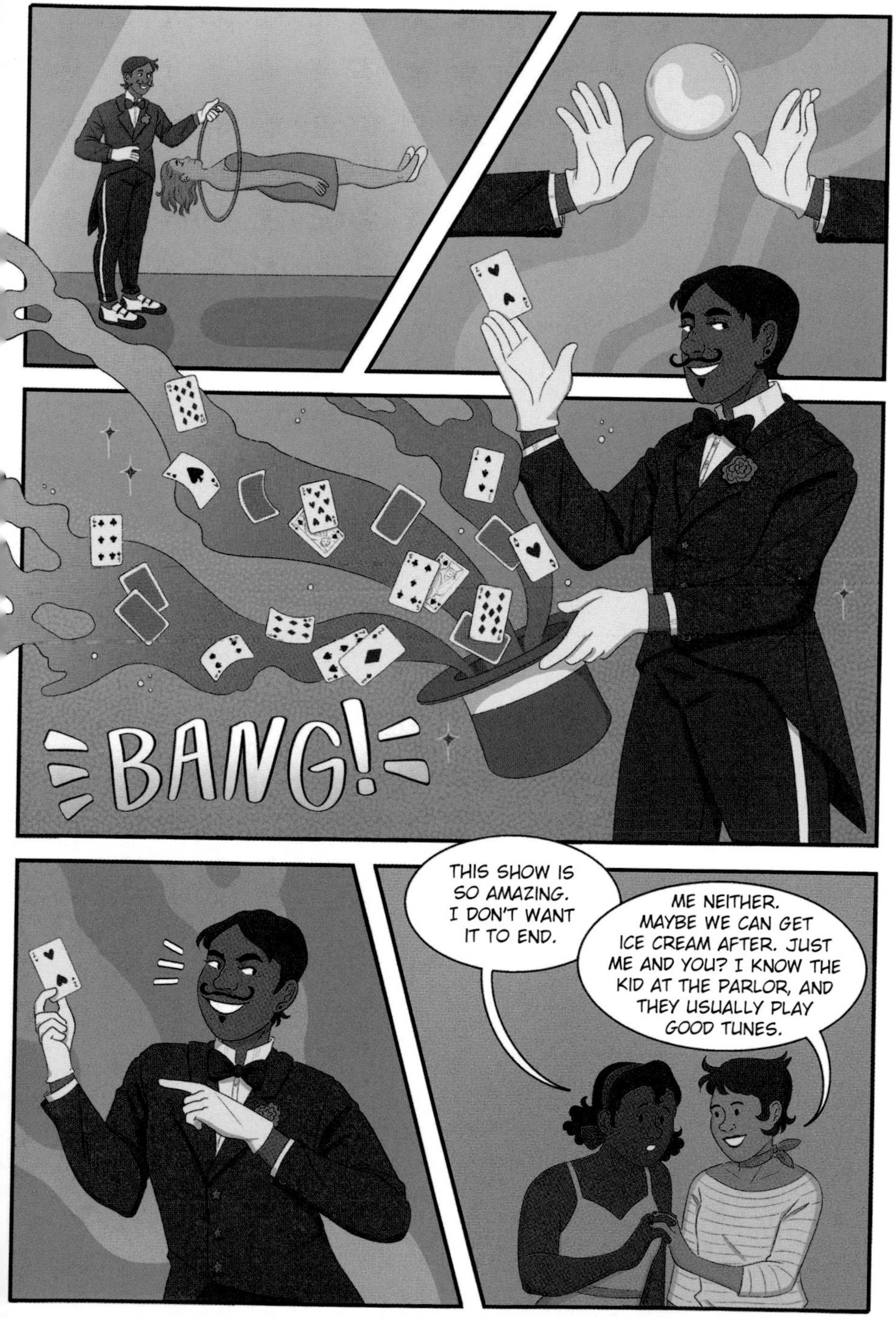
BANG!
THIS SHOW IS SO AMAZING. I DON'T WANT IT TO END.
ME NEITHER. MAYBE WE CAN GET ICE CREAM AFTER. JUST ME AND YOU? I KNOW THE KID AT THE PARLOR, AND THEY USUALLY PLAY GOOD TUNES.

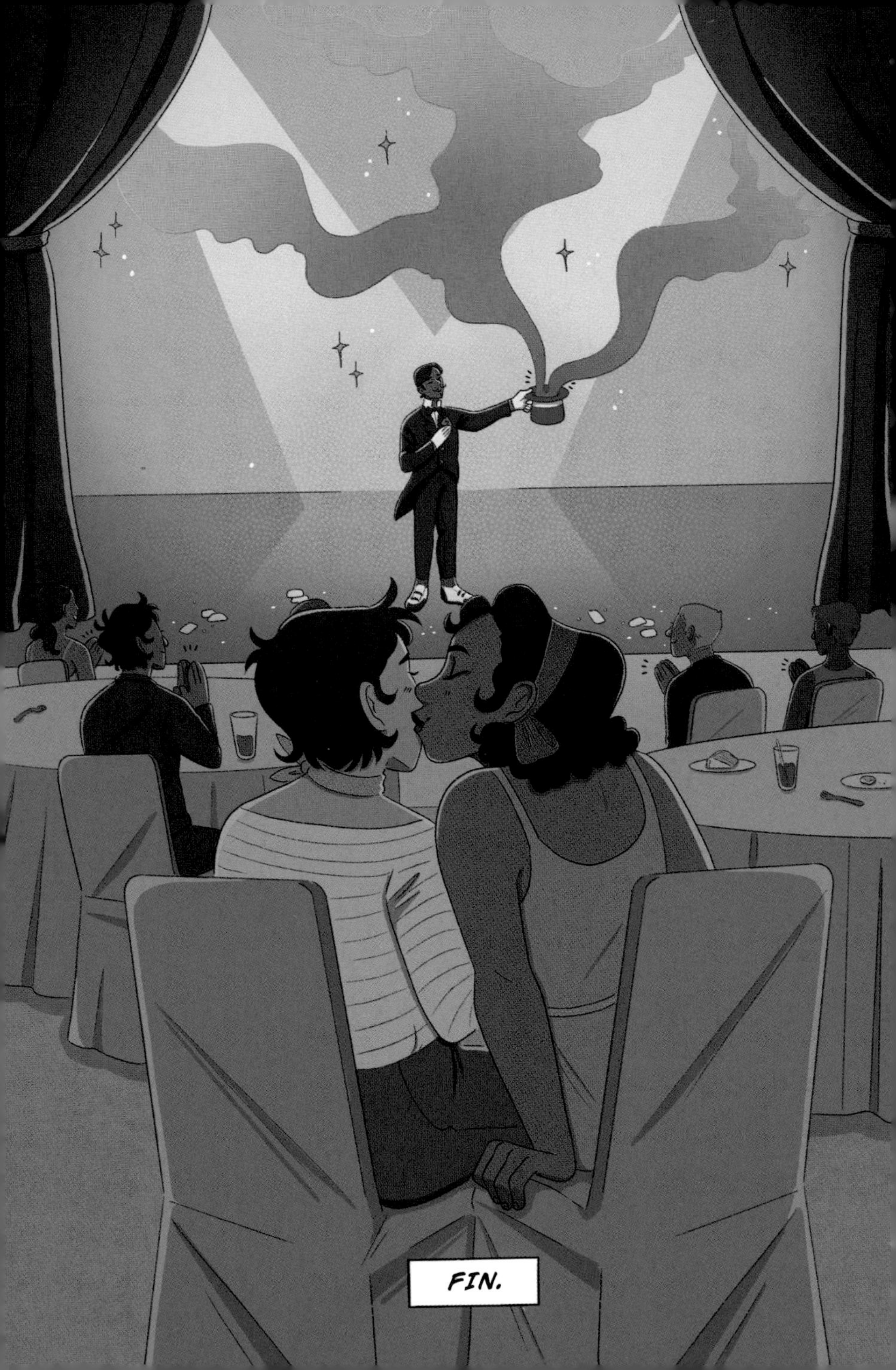
FIN.